Malibu, Calif.

The Golden Stallion and the Wolf Dog

By Rutherford G. Montgomery

The Golden Stallion
and the Wolf Dog

BY RUTHERFORD G. MONTGOMERY

Illustrated by PERCY LEASON

GROSSET & DUNLAP PUBLISHERS NEW YORK

PRINTED IN THE UNITED STATES OF AMERICA

For

KATHY MONTGOMERY

Contents

The Golden Stallion and the Wolf Dog

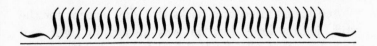

1. Outlaw

CHARLIE CARTER was bone-weary. It was a normal weariness to be expected after ten hours in the saddle. His hips ached and his leg muscles were sore. To add to his physical discomfort, Charlie was doing a slow burn. He prided himself on his judgment of horseflesh, and he had been wrong. Ace was not only an outlaw, he was the roughest-riding horse Charlie had ever known. When he got back to the Bar L, he'd have to admit to Tex Malone, the range boss, that he had been wrong about Ace. What angered him more than being wrong was a definite feeling that Ace was putting on the jolting, stiff-legged pace just to get even with Charlie for mastering him.

Charlie leaned forward and eased his knees. "You're going down the mountain to the rodeo boys," he said gruffly. "One thing you can do is buck."

3

Ace hadn't tried any tricks that day, except for the stiff, jolting lope, but he was always so tight and keyed up that Charlie had had to watch him closely for the first couple of hours. But now, after ten hours of riding, he figured Ace wouldn't feel up to any meanness, and Charlie had relaxed his watchfulness.

The wooded slopes of Bear Mountain dropped away below the bench Charlie was crossing. He had checked the ranch mares on the high range. Golden Boy, the palomino range stallion, was taking good care of them, but Charlie always checked every week. Today's check had revealed the presence of another stallion on the horse range. Golden Boy was unmarked, but there were signs of a fight—grass trampled and earth deep-pitted in a meadow. With Golden Boy in charge, there was little danger of a wild stallion stealing any of the mares. Charlie smiled as he imagined what had happened to the wild intruder when he had showed up. Golden Boy had been a wild horse himself, and he fought with the savage fury of a killer. At the moment Charlie was making a big circle of the range, hoping to sight the wild stallion. If Golden Boy had crippled the wild horse badly, Charlie would put him out of his misery with his saddle carbine.

Charlie had hoped to make a rope horse out of Ace. He was heavy through the chest, and had powerful legs. Ace had taken to roping at once. It was the only thing he did willingly and well. Shorty Spears, the Bar L horse wrangler, sided with Tex regarding Ace. He predicted that the outlaw would never make a safe rope horse.

"He'll come undone when you least expect it," he

had warned Charlie. "You'll tie onto a cow and he'll toss you high as a kite."

Ace swerved to swing around a huge boulder. They were entering the broken barren country above the Bar L range. Big rocks lay scattered about, with clumps of cherry and scrub oak growing between them. Ace snorted and slanted his ears forward. At that instant a small red cow broke cover and bounded down the slope. One glance showed Charlie that she was a maverick, an unbranded animal that had been missed during the calf roundup. Charlie pulled Ace around and set his spurs. Ace bolted after the cow. Charlie loosened his saddle rope and got set to shake out a loop. If he could rope the cow and hog-tie her, he'd build a sagebrush fire and brand her with the running iron he carried. She would be worth at least a hundred dollars to the Bar L.

Ace quickly closed in on the cow. Charlie rose in his stirrups and swung his rope. He gave Ace his head, sure the horse would come through in good form. But Ace did not play the game according to the rules. With a savage squeal he planted his feet and twisted sharply around, then humped his back and shot into the air. Charlie was standing up and off balance. He knew in an instant that he was going to be thrown, and grabbed for the saddle horn. His fingers missed the horn, and he felt himself falling. His right foot twisted as he went down, and he felt a hard jerk on his leg. His boot had somehow become wedged in the stirrup. Ordinarily, the shape of a riding boot keeps it from wedging, but this was one time in a thousand when a boot failed.

Charlie reached frantically for the Colt .45 he always carried when he rode a dangerous horse. His hand clutched at empty leather. The Colt had been jerked from its holster when Ace came undone. Charlie's head and shoulders hit the ground. His body bounced and hit again. Charlie gritted his teeth as he strained to pull himself up so that he could reach the imprisoned boot. Ace was lunging and kicking so wildly as he charged across the rocky ground that Charlie could not reach the stirrup. He knew that unless he freed his foot he would have less than a minute to live. He had once seen a man dragged by a crazy horse. The end had come quickly from a smashed skull. Charlie's head hit the ground again and he felt a wave of dizziness sweep over him. Pain shot through his body from his twisted leg to the back of his head. But he did not lose consciousness; he kept trying to pull himself forward and up. His head hit the ground again and lights exploded before his eyes. This is it, he thought dully, as his body went limp.

Suddenly his head stopped hitting the ground. He was lying still, and through the haze that swam before his eyes, he heard Ace snorting above him. He shook his head to clear it, and pushed with his hands in an effort to sit up. He managed to get into a half crouch. His head was clearing and he was able to see a little. What he saw did not make much sense. He wasn't sure, but he thought he was looking up at a big dog standing close to him. Charlie decided that it was a dog, though it looked exactly like a big gray wolf. The dog's tongue lolled out in a friendly manner. Charlie shook his head again and turned it. He saw a boy standing above him, looking anxiously down at him. The boy was hatless, and he had dark eyes and jet-black hair. He had a rope on Ace and was bearing down hard, choking the outlaw into submission. The boy's horse stood nearby with its head down.

"That was close, *amigo*," the boy said.

Charlie grinned weakly. "Too close," he agreed.

The boy had roped Ace and had dismounted, going down the rope steer-dogging fashion, so that he could free Charlie's trapped boot, which was still caught in the stirrup.

"I can hold him if you can work your boot loose," the boy said.

"I'll pry it loose." Charlie turned over and placed his free boot against the trapped instep. He pushed hard as Ace jerked and twisted. His foot came free. He sat looking down at the boot. A ripped seam showed why it had stuck. The rip had been small when Charlie started out, but it had opened up, exposing a flap of leather that had wedged his foot in the stirrup.

Charlie flexed his arms, then felt of his leg. His head ached, but otherwise he seemed to be sound and uninjured. He got slowly to his feet. Stepping close to Ace, he caught up the bridle reins.

"I'll take him now," he said. "Thanks for saving my neck."

"Better let me choke some sense into his head," the boy suggested.

Charlie laughed grimly. "I'll work some sense into him." He made it a rule never to let a horse master him. Now was the time to show Ace who was boss. The boy shook his head dubiously, but he released the pressure on the rope and Ace took a deep breath. Charlie freed the rope and got set to swing into the saddle.

"You going to get on him?" There was a look of admiration in the boy's dark eyes.

"What would you do?" Charlie asked.

"Get on and comb him down, I guess," the boy admitted.

Charlie smiled. He pulled Ace's head around, and held out a hand to the boy. "I'm Charlie Carter from the Bar L." The boy gripped Charlie's hand.

"I'm Pedro Martinez," he said with a shy smile. "No address."

"Stand by, Pedro," Charlie said. "After I've worked this hammerhead over, we'll talk."

Charlie swung into the saddle and dug his spurs deep. Ace snorted and lunged, but he did not buck. He knew that Charlie was ready for him and would give him a rough time if he fought back. Charlie sent the horse across the bench at a furious pace, swung him around, and sent him back. He had a feeling as they charged back across the mesa that Ace hadn't conceded a thing; he was just playing it smart. He pulled up beside Pedro and his dog, then dismounted. Ace shook himself and blew heavily. His eyes rolled white and his nostrils flared defiantly, but he stood ground-hitched, and did not try to run away. Charlie faced Pedro.

He noticed that the boy was watching him closely. He seemed to be trying to make up his mind about something. There was a wariness about him that re-

minded Charlie of a wild creature that was on the
alert for danger. Pedro wore no belt gun and there
was no rifle on his saddle. His pack was only a rolled
blanket which could not have concealed a very large
pack of grub or cooking pots or anything else. Yet
Pedro was a long way from any place where he could
get a meal without a gun. Pedro nodded toward the
dog.

"Shag and me are on the trail of a white stallion,"
he explained.

Charlie was interested. "The Bar L range stallion
has been fighting. Could be your horse is up here."

"He's up here," Pedro said eagerly. "But if he
fought with your stallion, he'd have taken over."

Charlie grinned. "He's quite a bit of horse?"

"He's the white stallion," Pedro said simply.

Charlie was puzzled for a moment until he remembered the stories he had heard and read about a fan-
tastic pacing white stallion. But the white stallion was
a legend from the past. There were many stories
written about him. Many men had hunted him, but
none had ever captured him.

"If he's the white stallion, he must be a hundred
years old," Charlie said with a wide smile.

Pedro did not smile, but an eager light came into his
eyes, and his words came fast. "There has been more
than one white stallion. Every so often one appears
from nowhere and makes himself king of the range.
Of this I am sure. This horse is the white stallion."

Pedro was so serious that Charlie did not laugh. He
was ready to admit that Pedro might have followed
a white stallion into the high country, but he was sure

that the horse was no phantom with invincible powers. Golden Boy had beaten him and routed him.

"You can stay at the Bar L while you hunt for your white stallion," Charlie said. "If we hit leather, we'll be home in time for a hot supper." He noticed Pedro's lips tighten when he mentioned food.

"Do you have near neighbors?" Pedro asked, his eyes searching Charlie's face.

"The Bar L is in an isolated valley. Our nearest neighbor lives twenty miles away." Charlie watched the reaction on Pedro's face. It was one of relief.

"I am very grateful," Pedro said.

"You saved my life," Charlie reminded him. "You are welcome to stay at the Bar L as long as you wish, and I'll help you catch your white stallion."

Pedro certainly needed another horse. The one he was riding was old and bony. Looking at the horse, Charlie wondered how the ancient fellow had managed to hold Ace. He suspected this boy was no ordinary horseman. Wherever he had learned to ride and rope, he had learned well. And yet, he could not be over sixteen years of age.

"With the white stallion I could ride fast and far," Pedro said. "I will be grateful if you will help me catch him. My horse is not fast, but he is wise and pretty strong." Pedro gave the old horse an affectionate look.

"It's a deal. First I have to find my hat and belt gun."

Pedro helped Charlie search for the hat and the gun. They found the hat at once, but finding the Colt

.45 took longer. It was Shag, the wolf dog, who scented it in a clump of sage and soapweed.

As Charlie approached Ace, the horse rolled his eyes, but he did not move when Charlie caught a stirrup and set his boot into it.

"I would not trust him," Pedro said, his eyes on the outlaw.

Charlie swung into his saddle and kept a tight rein on Ace. Pedro mounted his horse and they rode away at a fast trot. Pedro watched Ace with a thoughtful look in his eyes.

"I think he has a touch of loco poison," he said after they had traveled almost a mile.

"What makes you think he's a loco?" Charlie asked.

"On my father's ranch in Mexico we had trouble with the weed. He has the crazy stiff-legged gait the poison gives a horse." Pedro frowned as though he had said more than he should.

Charlie considered what Pedro had said. It was possible that Ace had been poisoned and was recovering from the effects. This would account for the sudden wild spells that came on at unexpected times. Pedro's mention of Mexico interested him, too.

"When you catch the white stallion, will you go back to Mexico?" he asked.

Pedro nodded. "I will go quickly." There was a worried look on the boy's face. The hunted look had returned. He glanced back, his eyes covering the sweep of the country above them.

He's running away from something, Charlie thought, but he did not question Pedro or try to get him to talk

There was a worried look on the boy's face

about his past. If Pedro was running away from something, that was his business. He liked the boy and felt
sure that he could not be mixed up in any crime. He
probably had borrowed the old horse he was riding.
Charlie did not recognize the brand. Pedro probably
planned to return the horse as soon as he was able to
catch an unbranded mount. Charlie smiled. Pedro
was certainly optimistic, planning to catch a wild
stallion with the mount he was riding.

They loped along, with Shag running ahead. The
dog ran with the long, easy strides of a wolf. Tex
would be furious when he saw the dog. Tex suspected
all dogs bigger than a terrier, especially wolf dogs.
He contended that every dog was a potential calf
killer. Charlie meant to be firm with Tex. Pedro and
Shag were guests and would be made welcome no
matter how Tex felt.

Pedro was silent for a long time. When they topped
the last ridge above the valley where the home spread
lay, he looked the place over carefully. The buildings
of the Bar L stood at the lower end of an expanse of
meadows. There was a rambling two-story house, built
of carefully selected pine logs, with a shake roof and
a fireplace chimney built out of river boulders. Below
the house stood a big barn built from milled lumber,
two large corrals, a bunkhouse and a saddle house.
Back of the barn was the feed lot with its racks and
shelter sheds. The whole valley was fenced and served
as pasture for the white-faced cows while they were
being held for calving, and to await the coming of
tall grass to the high benches above the ranch. After
the cows were off pasture, the meadows would be

flooded with water from Roaring River. In the fall, hay would be cut and stacked for winter use.

The scene was a familiar one to Charlie. He had been born in the big house. He had lived on the ranch all his life, except for winters spent in town while going to school. Pedro's eyes lighted up as he looked upon the scene.

"It is a beautiful ranch," he said softly.

"Do you live on a fine ranch in Mexico?" Charlie asked.

Pedro shook his head. "There is no ranch there any more. I have nothing in Mexico."

Charlie thought he was going to say more, but the boy remained silent, his thoughts well concealed by an expressionless face.

2. Cow Dog

Tex was at the corral when the boys rode in. He placed his hands on his hips and watched as Shag the dog trotted up to the corral gate and sat down. There was a bleak frown on Tex's face as he nodded to Charlie and Pedro. His glance rested on Pedro only for a moment, but the boy was watching Tex intently. Charlie dismounted and Pedro swung nimbly from his saddle.

"Pedro, meet Tex Malone, our ranch boss," Charlie said.

"It is a pleasure." Pedro smiled at Tex.

Tex just nodded his head and said nothing.

"Pedro is staying with us for a while," Charlie explained. "He's hunting a wild stallion."

"We don't allow any dogs on the ranch," Tex said flatly. "This dog is a wolf dog, the worst kind of calf killer."

"Shag is a trained cow dog," Pedro said quickly. "I will show you what he can do."

"He'll have to be chained or kept inside the barn," Tex retorted grimly.

Charlie flushed and his lips pulled into a tight line. Tex had been range boss since Charlie was a small boy, and he had never stopped bossing Charlie. He was about to tell Tex that the dog would have the run of the ranch when his father came out of the barn and joined them. Charlie introduced Pedro to his father. Grandby Carter smiled at the boy as they shook hands.

"Welcome to the Bar L, Pedro," he said.

Pedro smiled broadly. Grandby's warm welcome took the edge off Tex's coldness. Charlie decided this was the time to level with Tex regarding Ace.

"You were right about Ace, Tex." He met Tex's stare squarely. Tex wasn't hiding his feelings toward the dog. "He came undone today when I tried to rope a maverick heifer. He threw me and I got a boot hung up in a stirrup. I was in a bad way when Pedro showed up and dropped a rope on Ace."

Grandby looked at Charlie sharply, noting his torn shirt and scratched back and shoulders. "He dragged you?"

"Yes." Charlie laid a hand on Pedro's shoulder. "Pedro is a mighty smooth hand with a rope."

Tex had turned away and was watching Shag. He accepted Charlie's admission about Ace without a word. He had been proved right and would let it go at that.

"We are indebted to you, Pedro," Grandby said

warmly. "Make yourself at home on the Bar L as long as you wish to stay."

Tex faced Pedro. "You got Charlie out of a bad spot." His voice was level and Charlie knew Tex felt that if his advice had been taken, there would have been no trouble. "You're sure welcome, but something has to be done about that dog."

"Shag is a fine cattle dog," Pedro said quickly, looking hopefully up at Grandby. "He works cattle better than a mounted man."

"He's a fine-looking dog," Grandby agreed. "Has a strain of wolf in him, hasn't he?"

"His father was a famous lobo. Every cattleman in New Mexico tried to trap him or shoot him. There were rewards offered, but no one ever brought in his scalp." There was pride in Pedro's voice.

"That's just why that dog can't run loose here on the ranch," Tex snapped.

Pedro looked anxiously at Grandby. Grandby bent and rumpled the hair between Shag's ears. The dog whimpered eagerly and rubbed his head against Grandby's leg.

"You can give us a demonstration of Shag's work with cows." Grandby met Tex's hostile eyes. "He might make a good Bar L hand."

Pedro beamed. Charlie decided this was the time to settle the matter of Shag's freedom.

"He won't be chained," he said. "He gets to run."

"He will have the run of the ranch," Grandby agreed.

Tex turned on his heel and walked away toward the bunkhouse. Charlie felt irritated. He considered himself a partner with his father in running the ranch.

"Tex thinks he owns the spread," he said sharply.

Grandby smiled. "Tex has been with us a long time. He does have a stake in the Bar L." He looked at Pedro's old horse and shook his head. "He should be retired. How old is he?" He looked at Pedro.

"It is hard to tell by the teeth after twelve, but I would guess he is twenty," Pedro answered gravely.

Grandby nodded. "Put him out to grass. Charlie will wrangle you a horse. Now get unsaddled and give that pair a rubdown. Supper must be about ready."

Charlie and Pedro unsaddled and rubbed their horses down. Grandby waited for them. Ace acted like a thoroughly broken saddle animal. He meekly allowed Charlie to comb and brush his sweat-streaked flanks and belly. Charlie got grain for the pair, bringing ground meal for the ancient one. As he closed the corral gate, he said:

"Pedro thinks Ace may have a touch of loco weed."

Grandby looked at Ace thoughtfully. "He drifted up out of the desert. He could have gotten some of the weed down there. Our range is clean."

Grandby Carter had gone to considerable trouble and expense in eliminating poison weeds from his range. All his riders were always on the alert for dangerous plants. No loco had been found in recent years.

The boys walked to the house with Grandby. Shag marched ahead of them. He sniffed along the picket fence, and inspected everything. Charlie's mother was in the living room. Pedro's eyes moved first over the big room with its high-beamed ceiling and its giant fireplace and homey furniture, then he looked shyly at Ann Carter. She was small and looked frail beside her six-foot husband and her son who was an inch taller than his father.

"Pedro, meet my mother," Charlie said.

Pedro bowed low and his dark face flushed. He muttered something which sounded to Charlie like Spanish. Ann Carter laughed and held out both hands to Pedro. He took them and his face lighted up with a smile.

"Welcome to our home, Pedro," Ann said warmly. She turned to Charlie. "Where did you two meet?"

"Up near the breaks."

Then Charlie briefly told his mother how Pedro had rescued him. Before he finished, Ann's smile had faded. She shuddered and shook her head. Until a slight heart ailment had forced her to give up riding, Ann Carter had been an expert horsewoman. In her early married years she had ridden the range with Grandby when they could not afford to hire an extra hand. She knew the danger of being dragged by a bolting horse.

"You were lucky," she said to Charlie in a low voice. Then she turned to Pedro and impulsively slipped an arm around the boy. She planted a kiss on his cheek. "Thank you, Pedro, for being there."

Pedro fairly glowed. It was clear that she had won him completely. The thought struck Charlie that Pedro acted as though he had not known a mother's love and the comforts of home for a long time. There had been a hungry look on his face when he first entered the house. Ann turned and glanced out through the big front window. Shag was standing on the porch, looking into the room, his head cocked on one side, a broad, eager grin on his face.

"What a beautiful dog!" Ann exclaimed.

"His name is Shag, and he's a trained cow dog." Charlie laughed. "Tex is sure he's a killer and wanted to chain him to a post."

"Oh, no!" Ann Carter said quickly. "He's the sort of dog who needs space to run."

Pedro nodded his head eagerly. "He is a range dog," he explained. "I have trained him to be a wolf killer as well as a cattle dog." Pedro drew himself up proudly. "He is my only close friend."

"Not any more, Pedro." Ann spoke gently. "You have just made some close friends."

Pedro flushed and shuffled his feet. He looked down at his scuffed boots with their run-over heels. "I am grateful," he said in a low voice.

Mrs. Garrity, the cook, came hurrying in, wiping her hands on a gingham apron. Mrs. Garrity was a big motherly woman who bossed the household in true Irish fashion, with half humor and half stubbornness.

"Supper is dished up!" she announced.

"Put on an extra plate. And meet Pedro," Grandby Carter said. "He will be our guest for a while."

Mrs. Garrity looked Pedro over and clucked her tongue. "He needs fattening up," she observed. "Will Shorty be in for supper?" She directed the question to Charlie's father.

"He should be in. He was riding the north drift fence," Grandby answered.

Charlie smiled broadly. For years Mrs. Garrity had been interested in Shorty, keeping an eye on him at all times. Shorty was wary. He liked his bachelor freedom. He had decided to quit the Bar L several times in order to escape, but Mrs. Garrity's cooking always made him change his mind.

Shorty came in with Tex and they washed up. At supper Pedro tried not to show how hungry he was. But he let Mrs. Garrity heap his plate twice with roast beef, mashed potatoes, and green peas. They all noticed Pedro's appetite, but no one made any comment. Shorty was very much interested in Charlie's bout with Ace.

"You better give that hoss up as a bad one," he advised. "I sort of agree with Pedro that he's a loco. Anyway, I'm dead sure he's a bad apple."

"If he's loco, he'll get over it," Charlie argued stubbornly.

"I'm sending him out with the five head we're selling to the Circle T," Grandby said firmly. "I'll toss him in as a bonus. The Circle boys go in for rodeo stock. He ought to make a good bucker."

"There is no need to take any chances with a bad horse," Ann agreed. "We have plenty of good horses."

"Hope I draw him at the cattlemen's show this fall," Charlie said with a grin. "I've about got his style figured out."

Ann smiled at her son. "Ellen will arrive next week and we want you to be in one piece. She'll want to ride all over the ranch the first day."

Charlie flushed and frowned. Ellen Sprague had been spending her summers on the ranch for several years. She and Charlie understood each other. He liked to have her for a companion. But his mother always made it look as though they were sweethearts. Charlie wasn't sure he felt that way about Ellen or that she had any special feeling for him. She could make him jealous, and he liked to have her with him on long rides, but he wasn't admitting anything. He caught Pedro's eyes on him. There was a twinkle in their dark depths.

With supper over, Pedro hovered near the kitchen door. Mrs. Garrity came into the dining room. Pedro bowed. "The dinner was very good." Pedro hesitated and seemed to be gathering his courage. "If there are some scraps, I could take them to Shag," he said.

Mrs. Garrity laughed. She took Pedro by the arm and guided him into the kitchen. She steered him to the back door. Looking out through the screen door, Pedro saw Shag busily bolting a meal of beef and potatoes. Pedro's eyes opened wide. Shag was not feasting on scraps. Mrs. Garrity had cut him a liberal piece of roast and heaped mashed potatoes and gravy over it.

"But—so much good food," Pedro protested.

Mrs. Garrity laughed heartily. "I heard what you did for Charlie, son. You and your dog get the best of everything there is around this kitchen."

Pedro opened the door and stepped out. He knelt beside Shag. He lowered his head, but Mrs. Garrity did not miss the mistiness in his eyes. She closed the back door and attacked the dishes stacked in the sink, addressing some pointed remarks to them.

"That boy's been without folks too long. Needs more than beef and spuds."

Charlie walked out on the front porch and sat on the railing. Presently Pedro and Shag appeared. Pedro sat beside Charlie while Shag stretched out at his feet. Charlie noticed that Shag had a crippled forepaw; two toes were missing.

"Was Shag caught in a steel trap?" he asked.

"He stepped into a trap while he was trailing a wolf," Pedro explained. "I was far back on the trail, and he had torn off his toes getting out of the trap before I got to him. It is a wolf trick," he added with a smile.

"Did you get the wolf?" Charlie asked. He was watching Pedro and thinking that for a boy so young he had done a great many things.

"Shag caught up with him. The wolf turned on Shag when he thought he was in a good spot for a kill. I guess that old wolf had killed many dogs." Pedro smiled. "I found Shag waiting for me on a ledge. The body of the wolf was lying at the foot of the ledge." Pedro looked down fondly at his dog. "I would like to have seen that fight."

"Do you think Shag would ever make up with a she-wolf?" Charlie asked.

"Yes," Pedro answered truthfully. "He would run with her under the mating moon. He probably would kill any sons she had, and after the run was over, if she tried to pull down a calf, he would turn on her."

Charlie decided that Pedro wasn't the sort of person who deluded himself; he thought straight. It would be great sport helping Pedro catch the white stallion.

"Tomorrow I'll show you a real stallion," Charlie said. "A wild one we trapped and gentled a bit."

"We must catch the white stallion before he hurts your horse," Pedro said gravely.

Charlie laughed. "Golden Boy can take care of himself in a fight."

"But this is no ordinary stallion," Pedro protested. "We may not be able to catch him at all. This is a pacing white stallion. It can be no other than the white stallion come back to be king again." Pedro's eyes glowed with the excitement that gripped him.

Charlie did not argue. In the morning he would show Pedro a real stallion. He admitted to himself that he was eager to see the mystery horse, but he was sure that the white one would not measure up to the golden stallion who was master of the Bar L herd of mares. He started telling Pedro the story of how they had captured the golden stallion and tamed him. Pedro nodded his head a number of times. When Charlie finished, Pedro said:

"He must be a great horse."

But Charlie knew he wasn't convinced that Golden Boy would be any match for the white stallion.

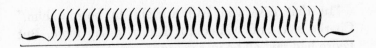

3. The Rival

PEDRO AND CHARLIE left the ranch early. The sun had not risen, but the sky was filled with light. Pedro was riding Diamond, a horse Ann Carter rode on the rare occasions when she felt she had to get back into the saddle again. But he insisted upon trailing his own horse. He was perfectly honest about his reason.

"I borrowed this horse. When we get into high country, I will turn him loose and he will go home." Pedro glanced back at the horse. "The owner will not mind at all. I worked with him at one time. We trapped wild horses."

Charlie made no comment. Borrowing a horse was stealing a horse, in his book. Pedro seemed to sense his feeling. There was a hint of defiance in his voice when he spoke again.

"The horse should have been mine."

"In that case you had a right to borrow him," Charlie said and waited for Pedro to say more. But Pedro had said all he was going to say about his former partner.

With Shag running far ahead, they loped across the meadows. They came to a herd of white-faced steers scattered along the slopes of a deep ravine. Pedro pulled Diamond to a halt.

"Would you like to see Shag work?" he asked.

Charlie nodded. He spoke to Trey Spot, who was restless and eager to push on. The mare shook her head impatiently and champed at her bit. Pedro slipped two fingers into his mouth and whistled. Shag was on a ridge above. He halted and looked down. Pedro whistled again, and Shag came bounding down the slope. As the dog drew near, Pedro waved an arm toward the steers.

"Round them up, Shag!" he shouted.

Shag whirled and raced away. He had been watching the steers and was ready to bunch them. He swung around the steers at the upper end of the ravine. They saw him coming, and to them he was a wolf. They ran from him and he pushed them toward another group of steers. Racing with long, easy strides, he circled back and forth, crowding the animals together and heading them toward the spot where Charlie and Pedro were waiting. Several spirited youngsters tried to bolt and escape, but Shag cut them off, leaping at their muzzles, his fangs flashing. He did not touch the flaring nostrils, but his fangs came so close that the steers whirled and charged back to the herd. Working their heels, Shag pushed the bunched herd up the

slope. When he reached the top, he whirled around
the herd and brought them to a halt.

"Perfect!" Charlie shouted.

Pedro whistled and Shag trotted away from the
steers. He bounded toward the boys and leaped up
against Pedro's stirrup. The steers stood staring for
a few minutes, then started to scatter. Shag whirled.
He looked up at Pedro, then toward the steers.

"That is all, Shag. Let them go," Pedro said. Shag
turned his back on the steers.

"I believe he understands every word you say,"
Charlie said.

"When we are alone, I talk to him a great deal,"
Pedro answered. "I think he understands much that
I say."

"How is he with big steers and bulls?" Charlie asked.

"I have seen him handle an angry bull." Pedro
laughed. "The bull suffered from a sore nose for sev-

eral days. If he has to be tough, he can really use his fangs."

"He'd sure be handy at roundup time. He'd take the place of a couple of line riders."

Pedro bent down to pat the dog's head. Diamond shied away, but Shag jumped high to receive the pat. "Good boy," Pedro said.

They headed up along a steep trail which led through Roaring River Canyon. The canyon was narrow and its sheer walls rose a thousand feet, so that the sun never penetrated to the river bed. The wild scene roused Shag and he raced ahead, as though looking for a hidden enemy. Near the top the boys halted to give their horses a breathing spell.

"This is a beautiful place," Pedro said. He was looking back into the shadowy depths of the canyon. The roar of the white water tumbling below floated up like music.

"Most folks do not like it," Charlie said. "They get out of the canyon as fast as they can."

Pedro laughed softly. "I like it—the feel of the dark places and the music of the river."

Charlie understood how Pedro felt. He liked to ride slowly up through the canyon. Shag came racing back as they started on. His tongue was hanging out, and he was panting. Charlie grinned down at the big dog.

"It sort of gets Shag, too," he observed.

After climbing out of the canyon, they rode across a wide bench which sloped gently up to a belt of spruce and fir. Pedro began checking the country above and below, watching the small parks and the narrow alleys between the trees. Charlie watched him closely. It was plain to him that Pedro was an expert wild-horse hunter. He wondered how long Pedro had been riding and roping. The thought prompted him to ask.

Pedro grinned. "I have ridden horses since I was five years old." He paused and seemed to be remembering back. "I was ten when I really started working horses, that is, the unbroken ones." Charlie waited for him to go on, but Pedro had said all he wanted to say about his past.

Pedro slipped the lead rope from around the neck of the old horse and turned him loose on a high ridge. He slapped the old fellow's rump with the rope and watched the horse trot away, down the slope toward a grassy meadow. Charlie said nothing as Pedro rode up beside him.

They reached the timber, and from there on, they passed parks and meadows surrounded by heavy timber. This was ideal horse country. There was deep cover close at hand on all sides. It was country Golden Boy liked, because he was still a wild stallion in many ways. Charlie slowed their pace and they halted often inside the woods to study parks and meadows. They were nearing the rock-strewn breaks when they sighted Golden Boy and the mares. The stallion stood on a knoll watching the mares feeding in a tall-grass meadow. His head was up and his blond mane and tail flowed in the wind. Charlie glanced at Pedro. The boy's eyes were wide open and filled with wonder and admiration.

"How do you like him?" Charlie asked.

"He's as big as the white stallion." There was a note

of awe in Pedro's voice. "We must not let them fight. One of them would be killed."

Charlie thought of the battle signs he had spotted the previous day. He hoped they would not find a crippled white stallion. His eyes ran over the herd of mares and he frowned as he checked them. He checked a second time and knew that four of the mares were missing. The four missing mares were horses that Grandby Carter had bought as racing stock. Charlie decided that when they found the white stallion, he would not be crippled, and that the four mares would be with him. He whistled sharply as he headed Trey Spot into the meadow. The mare whinnied eagerly.

Up on the knoll Golden Boy whirled about. He shook his head, then trotted toward the two riders.

"He may make a pass at Diamond!" Charlie warned.

Pedro laughed. "That I would like much to see." But he shook out a length of rope and swung it slowly. Trey Spot moved ahead and Pedro let Diamond drop behind. The big gelding was willing to keep his distance from Golden Boy. He had felt the sharp teeth of the stallion on several occasions. Golden Boy halted close to Trey Spot and extended his muzzle. Trey Spot nickered as their noses met.

"She has a crush on the big boy," Charlie said, and laughed.

Golden Boy edged away from Trey Spot. He had no desire to be caught and saddled, as he often was when Charlie visited the herd. Charlie saw that Golden Boy was marked on the neck and shoulders.

The scars were fresh and looked very much like teeth marks.

"They have been fighting," Pedro observed. There was a note of worry in his voice.

"We'll go look for your white stallion," Charlie said. "I think he's stolen four of our ranch mares."

They rode away and Golden Boy followed them to the edge of the timber. When he halted, he called to Trey Spot and she answered him. But he did not move out of sight of the herd, and soon galloped back to stand guard over it.

Charlie knew the country well, and was sure he could go straight to a spot any wild stallion would select as a safe feed ground. The horse would want plenty of timber and a deep arroyo into which he could stampede his herd if they were discovered. Charlie and Pedro pushed on into the high country, and as they moved upward, they were more careful to keep to cover at all times. Pedro called Shag in and had the dog follow Diamond. They checked every park as they skirted it. Now they were so high that the spruce and the fir trees were beginning to thin out. They had entered scrub growth before they came upon horse tracks. They found them along a stream which crossed a small park. As they sat looking down at the tracks, Pedro spoke softly.

"His tracks are here."

Charlie looked at a set of deep imprints close to the water. They were large and had been made by an unshod horse. He nodded but said nothing. They moved on until they came to the edge of a long park that broke off into a deep arroyo which became a canyon less than a mile below. At the upper end of the park they spotted a band of horses. Charlie counted eight head, and even at a distance he knew that four of them were Bar L mares, his father's racing stock. It took them five minutes to spot the white stallion. He was standing inside a spruce grove. Charlie wanted a closer look at the horse, so he headed Trey Spot up through the timber. Pedro dropped behind him. Shag sensed the tension and started testing the air eagerly.

When they were fifty yards from where the white stallion stood, Charlie turned Trey Spot toward the edge of the woods and halted just inside cover. They now had an excellent view of the stallion. He was as tall and as heavy as Golden Boy, but his legs were longer, and Charlie had an idea he was faster than the palomino. He was pure white without a single dark marking. He had a magnificent head, and a proud way of holding it. Charlie heard Pedro suck in his breath. A dead calm had settled over the scene. Not a hair in the stallion's mane or tail stirred. As he watched the big horse, Charlie knew he was going to go all out to help Pedro catch him. Pedro had first claim, but Charlie itched to get his hands on the big fellow.

As they watched, a breeze came flowing up from below. It stirred the needles on the spruce as it passed, and it carried the scent of the two horses and their riders to the flaring nostrils of the white stallion. Instantly the big fellow whirled. With a savage scream he charged down upon the mares, his ears back, his teeth bared. Charlie was amazed at his speed, but he was more amazed as he realized that the stallion was not galloping, he was pacing as smoothly as a stable-trained racer. It was impossible, and yet he had to believe his eyes. For a moment he almost believed this horse was a phantom. Then he stirred himself. He was between the stallion and the mares. Giving Trey Spot her head, he sent her racing across the meadow. The four wild mares were well trained. The moment the stallion screamed, they charged toward the rim of the arroyo. The ranch mares lifted their heads uncertainly and hesitated.

In that brief moment Charlie was between the ranch mares and the four wild horses heading for the arroyo. Pedro rode at his side, swinging his rope and shouting. Shag was racing to meet the white stallion. The stallion saw that he was outwitted. He slashed out with his forefeet at Shag, who was darting back and forth in front of him, then he swerved and raced after the four wild mares. The escaping mares plunged and slid down the steep side of the arroyo, with the stallion lashing their rumps with teeth and hoofs. Pedro and Charlie sat watching the wild scene. After the herd had disappeared into the canyon below, Charlie headed the ranch mares across the meadow toward lower country.

"Looks as if the two big boys have signed an armed truce!" he shouted to Pedro as they galloped along.

Pedro nodded and grinned. He was full of dreams and plans for catching the white stallion. Charlie was curious as to how Pedro planned to capture the horse. His experience with wild stallions had taught him a great deal. He decided that he had better have a talk with Pedro.

One thing was clearly evident to Charlie. The armed truce between the two would not last. In the end there would be a battle to the death. Golden Boy had destroyed Big Red, and Big Red had been a veteran so powerful and savage that he had reigned for a long time. Charlie had learned how tough Big Red was when he roped the stallion after ambushing him. That encounter had almost ended Charlie's riding career. It had crippled him so badly that he had not been able to ride for a year. Pedro might think he knew all about wild horses, but Charlie doubted that he had ever dropped a rope on a Big Red or a Golden Boy and tried to choke him into submission. He looked at Pedro. The boy had a dreamy, faraway look in his eyes, and he was smiling.

"How will you go about taking him?" he asked.

Pedro blinked his eyes as though shaking off a dream. The question seemed to surprise him. "The ambush. I'll rope him and choke him down." To Pedro it was as simple as catching a scrub on the mesas of New Mexico.

"I once dropped a rope on a wild stallion called Big Red," Charlie said. "Big Red didn't fight the rope. He came at me and smashed my horse. I was lucky. I only spent six months on crutches, and another six learning to ride again."

"What happened to Big Red?" Pedro asked.

"Golden Boy crippled him so badly that he was pulled down by wolves during the first blizzard that year." Charlie spoke slowly, remembering how he had come upon the stripped bones of the former king.

"That is the way of the wolf," Pedro said musingly. "The young and the cripples. Perhaps it is nature's way of making the young strong and of ending the troubles of the weak ones." He smiled at Charlie. "How did you catch Golden Boy?"

"The same way we will catch your white stallion, with a corral trap. It will take time and we'll have to get at it before those two have a showdown. I think the white stallion is just coming into maturity, and is trying his power for the first time. That may work in our favor, giving us more time."

"I have helped to catch hundreds of wild horses but never a big stallion," Pedro said thoughtfully. "The stallions I have taken were scrubs that Diamond could easily handle. I think you speak wisely. I think the white stallion would fight madly."

Charlie grinned. "Good," he said. "We'll start planning. The first thing to do is to study the grazing habits of our horse and the avenues of escape he uses. He'll work out a pattern which he will very likely follow. When we have a sure route, we'll build our trap."

"You offer to do much for me," Pedro said gravely.

"I owe you a lot, and besides I have Golden Boy and the Bar L mares to think about. Do you know how a wild stallion is handled if he cannot be driven off or caught?"

"No," Pedro admitted.

"Tex would settle the matter very simply—with a

Winchester high-power rifle." Charlie spoke grimly.

A look of horror came into Pedro's face. "He would shoot such a horse?"

"That is the surest way of ridding the range of a dangerous stallion. It's quick and costs only the price of one cartridge. No work building a corral and no time lost waiting for a chance to stampede a herd." Charlie smiled at Pedro. "That was what I was supposed to do with Big Red."

Pedro's frown changed to a smile. "You would never shoot a fine horse."

"No," Charlie admitted. "I guess I'm just not built that way."

They spent the rest of the day scouting the territory where the white stallion grazed his mares, being careful not to flush the herd. From now on, they would observe only from a distance, and learn the habits of the leader. They had their lunch on the bank of a clear, cold stream, and headed for home three hours before sunset.

Pedro was excited, but there were times when the boy settled into a brooding mood and the hunted look returned to his face. When they reached the corral, Tex, Shorty, and Grandby were there caring for their horses. Charlie told them how Shag had rounded up the steers. Grandby and Shorty were very much impressed, but Tex remained grimly silent.

"You have to see it to appreciate it," Charlie said enthusiastically.

"I have seen a good cow dog work," Shorty said. "I knew one that you couldn't have bought for five hundred dollars. Cal Winters of the Lazy K down in Texas owned him."

"We saw Pedro's white stallion," Charlie said. He didn't say that the wild horse had stolen four Bar L mares which he and Pedro had recovered.

"Is he a pacer?" Shorty asked quickly.

"He's a natural pacer," Charlie answered, and waited for the protests and arguments to come.

"He is big and very fast," Pedro added.

"You are sure he isn't branded?" Grandby asked.

"Not a mark on him." Charlie was positive. "You know he's a wild horse as soon as you see him."

"I better ride up and take care of him," Tex said grimly.

"We're going to trap him." Charlie gave Tex a defiant look.

"What will we do with another half-wild stallion?" Grandby asked.

"He's to be Pedro's horse," Charlie replied.

Grandby considered thoughtfully. He was aware of the debt they owed Pedro, and he was a horse lover. He disliked shooting a good horse to get rid of it. "There may be trouble between this horse and Golden Boy," he said.

"It is sure to come," Charlie admitted. "But we'll get busy and trap him before there is any trouble. Golden Boy has beaten him once, so he's apt to lay off for a while."

"We can't give you much help, and I'll need you part of the time for ranch work." Grandby spoke slowly, but Charlie knew the issue was settled. He and Pedro could go ahead with their plans to trap the white stallion.

That evening at supper Ann handed Charlie an airmail letter. Charlie tried not to grab eagerly for it. He knew it was from Ellen, telling him when she would arrive. It would be fun having Ellen help him in the wild-horse hunt. He started to tuck the letter into his pocket, but his mother stopped him.

"Read it," she urged. "We are all eager to know when Ellen will arrive."

The letter had been delayed because there was no regular mail delivery to the ranch. It had arrived at Cedar Bank a week ago. Ann and Grandby had gotten the mail while in town for supplies that day. Charlie read the letter carefully, lingering over the parts intended only for himself. When he finished, he smiled at his mother.

"Ellen is flying in. She'll arrive by Mountain Air Liner tomorrow afternoon at three."

"Wonderful!" Ann exclaimed. "You and Pedro can drive in and meet her."

Pedro looked down at his plate and said nothing. After supper when he and Charlie were alone on the front porch, he said:

"I do not wish to go to Cedar Bank."

He offered no reason for not wanting to go to town, and Charlie did not press him. Charlie had a feeling that Pedro did not want to be seen in town. If he was hiding from trouble, Charlie wanted to help him, but he could not unless Pedro asked him to.

"You can ride up to the high country and scout out

a good stand of aspen poles we can use to build the corral," he said, and smiled at Pedro.

Pedro returned the smile gratefully. He got to his feet and walked around to the kitchen door to make sure Shag had been fed. Mrs. Garrity had set out a plate of meat and bones. Again Pedro frowned. Ever since he was a small boy, Pedro had struggled to get enough to eat. Shag had always rustled rabbits and ground squirrels for food. Pedro could not help feeling that the food Shag was eating should have been used to feed hungry people. Shag was able to rustle for himself.

Pedro slept in Charlie's room on a single bed which had been installed for Charlie's guests from town. As he settled down in bed that night, Charlie was aware that Pedro was lying awake, staring at the ceiling. He discovered this when he awoke at midnight after having a disturbing dream. He didn't speak to Pedro, but he could see the boy's face in a band of moonlight coming through the window.

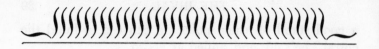

4. Ellen

BEFORE LEAVING for Cedar Bank, Charlie outfitted Pedro for his trip into the high country. He put an ax and a saw into the pack. Mrs. Garrity fixed a lunch.

Shorty was upset because fence mending kept him from going with Pedro. They had talked a lot about the white stallion. Shorty knew all the legends written about the phantom horse of the plains, and he and Pedro were ready to believe the wild horse on the range was a descendant of the pacing stallion made famous in stories and tales. Shorty argued that many men had written accounts of chasing the pacing stallion. There were authentic records of rewards posted for his capture. Shorty had taken time to ride up into the breaks for a look at the white stallion but had missed him.

Charlie did not argue, but he was amused. He had

seen the stallion and he was a magnificent animal, but he wasn't any ghost.

Tex was still nursing his distrust of Shag. Before Pedro rode away, he spoke to the boy about his dog. "Keep an eye on that dog. There'll be trouble if I find any calves pulled down!"

Pedro looked at Tex. "You have wolves on your range," he said evenly, meeting Tex's eyes squarely. "I have seen the sign."

"They never come as far down as the calf pasture," Tex said shortly.

Pedro shrugged his shoulders. "I'll keep Shag with me," he promised.

Tex mounted his bay and rode away. Charlie shook his head. "Tex just can't trust a dog." He smiled at Pedro. "Remember, we're trapping the big fellow, so don't try dabbing a rope on him."

"I will remember," Pedro said.

After Pedro rode away, Charlie put gas and oil into the Buick. To him a car was a necessity, not a conveyance to be enjoyed. He took care of its mechanical needs, and drove it to town because the distance to the county seat was a half day's ride on a horse. Also, Ellen would have baggage, which would have called for a pack horse. Charlie grinned as he pictured himself trailing a saddle horse and a pack animal into Cedar Bank and out to the airport. The people in the county seat would have thought it odd.

He asked his mother to go with him, but hoped she would refuse, which she did. It was always good fun to ride back to the ranch alone with Ellen. She lived in the East, and her enthusiasm when she returned to the ranch always pleased Charlie. He was so proud of the mountain setting that he got a big kick out of her excitement.

Charlie drove fast until he reached the twisting climb up to the divide. He put the car into second gear and let it grind its way to the top. Speed was of little concern to him; he was geared to the speed of a good horse. As he rode along, his thoughts kept going back to Pedro. In the short time he had known the boy he had formed a strong liking for him.

The long downgrade drive from the pass was over switchback gravel road, most of it built by Grandby Carter and a few ranchers with the assistance of the county road machinery. One lonely telephone wire followed the road. The wire was supported by pine poles set by the ranchers. It was a party line, and the phones were the old-fashioned kind that had to be cranked. But it was a vital link between the isolated ranchers and the doctors and the lawyers and the cattle buyers who lived in the county seat.

Charlie arrived in Cedar Bank an hour before the plane was due. The airport was a fifteen-minute drive from Main Street, so Charlie had time to do a little shopping. He went to the hardware store and bought a box of cartridges for his saddle rifle and one for his Colt. After that, he visited the harness shop and left his ripped boot to be repaired. Then he went to the poolroom, which had a refreshment bar. A Coke with chopped ice was a luxury he always enjoyed when he was in town. He avoided the drugstore with its soda counter because there was usually a bevy of town girls there who knew him from high school and who were always curious about a cowboy. In the poolroom he would meet cow hands and ranchers, the sort of people he felt comfortable with.

There were a number of men in the poolroom, some drinking at the bar, others lounging in the battered chairs along the wall. No one was playing pool. Charlie ordered his tall Coke and started sipping it. A hand from the Slash L came over and Charlie bought him a Coke.

"How's tricks out at the Bar L?" Mike asked.

"Same as always." Charlie liked Mike. The cow hand had worked for his father a number of times, usually at roundup or dipping time.

"In to pick up a guest?" Mike grinned. He knew Ellen came to stay at the ranch every summer, and he noted that Charlie was dressed up—wearing a new hat and a new bandanna. Charlie grinned back at Mike.

"Ellen's coming in by plane," he admitted.

Mike nodded. "Going to be needing an extra hand for dipping?"

"I don't know," Charlie said thoughtfully. "A youngster who is mighty handy with a horse and rope drifted in a few days back. A Mexican boy from New Mexico."

The man next to Mike, a lean, unshaven man with close-set eyes, turned his head and stared at Charlie, then gave his attention to his drink. Charlie hardly noticed the man. He had never seen him before, but put him down as a saddle tramp drifting through the country.

"They often make fine hands. Always mighty good

with horses," Mike commented. "But if he drifts on, I could use a few days' work."

Charlie glanced at the clock over the bar. It was time to drive out to the airport. He filled his mouth with chopped ice and mumbled to Mike, "Be seeing you. If Dad needs another hand, I'll call you."

Charlie parked outside the long shed which served as a shelter at the landing strip. He sat in the car waiting for the arrival of the plane. Presently he heard the drone of its motors and a few minutes later the small two-engine liner swept over a ridge and slanted down toward the strip, its silver wings gleaming in the sun. The plane's wheels hit the runway with a spurting puff of yellow dust, and it bounced in toward the shed, coming to rest with its idling engines whipping up clouds of dust behind it.

The only passenger to alight was Ellen Sprague. Her short corn-colored hair was whipped by the breeze blowing across the field. Her blue eyes danced as Charlie hurried forward to meet her.

"Hello," she greeted him, holding out two slim hands.

Charlie took her hands. "Hello," he said, and his voice left no doubt that he was glad to see her.

Ellen stood looking up at the mountains. Charlie glanced past her and saw that the airport attendant was grinning at him. He quickly dropped Ellen's hands and muttered:

"I'll get your stuff."

"Each time they look more beautiful," Ellen said eagerly.

"They're the same old mountains," Charlie assured her quickly. He scowled at the attendant.

The attendant moved out to get Ellen's bags. Charlie met him and took the baggage. He was prepared for the fellow if he made a crack. The attendant grinned at him.

"Have to have baggage checks," he said.

Ellen fished the checks from her handbag and handed them over. Charlie loaded the suitcases into the back seat and held the door open for Ellen. When she was seated, he asked, "Hungry?"

"No," she answered with a smile. "Let's leave at once. I can hardly wait to see the ranch again."

"There are some real surprises waiting for you," Charlie assured her as he started the engine and headed the car toward town. They turned off on the mountain road leading to the pass. Charlie didn't seem to realize that the road was straight for two miles. He drove just under forty. As they rode through the foothills and on up the twisting road to the pass, Charlie told Ellen about Pedro and the white stallion. Her excitement grew as the story unfolded. When Charlie finished, she exclaimed:

"I'm in on the capture of the white stallion!"

"We've been counting on your help," Charlie assured her. "I'm a little worried about Pedro—the way he came to us, and little things. Something seems to be bothering him. But you'll like him. He's a straight shooter, so I'm not worried about his being in any serious trouble."

"He may have run away from home," Ellen said.

"I don't think he's had a home for a long time," Charlie commented thoughtfully. He roused himself and pushed down on the gas pedal. They were nearing the pass and the Buick was laboring in second gear.

On the divide Charlie let the car hesitate a moment before rolling into the sharp curves below. Ellen caught her breath. Roaring River Valley spread below them like a vast green carpet, framed with deep blue where the pines and the spruce fringed the meadowland.

"Home," she said softly, and gave Charlie a quick shy glance.

"Home," Charlie repeated, but he wasn't able to look at Ellen, and knew his neck and ears were red. For a short distance he took the curves at a speed higher than his usual way of driving.

As they turned into the poplar-shaded driveway leading to the ranch house, Shag came bounding out to meet them. That meant Pedro had returned from the high range. Charlie braked the car to a stop before the front gate. Ann Carter came down the path. Charlie looked for Pedro, but he wasn't around. Ellen jumped out of the car and rushed to embrace Charlie's mother. Charlie stood by, beaming, until Ann reminded him of Ellen's bags.

When they entered the house, Grandby came out of the small room he used as an office. He slipped an arm around Ellen. "Welcome to the hill country," he said.

"I'm so excited I'm about to pop." Ellen laughed up into Grandby's face.

"Where's Pedro?" Charlie asked.

"In the kitchen," his mother answered. "I think that Mrs. Garrity baited him into her domain with fresh doughnuts and milk."

"Sounds like a spot for you and me," Charlie said, with a grin for Ellen.

They went through the dining room to the kitchen. Pedro sat at the kitchen table with a big glass of milk in one hand and a doughnut in the other. Before him was a tray heaped high with freshly cooked dough-nuts. Pedro set his glass and doughnut down and jumped to his feet. Before Charlie could introduce him, he made a bow and smiled shyly at Ellen.

"Ellen," he said, "I am honored to meet you."

Ellen repressed a laugh as she held out her hand. Pedro took it but let go of it very quickly. "Charlie has told me all about you, Pedro."

Pedro's dark eyes searched her face intently for a moment before glancing quickly at Charlie.

"It was all good. I add my thanks for what you did for Charlie," Ellen said.

"It was nothing," Pedro answered, but his face lighted up eagerly.

They sat at the table and ate doughnuts and drank cold milk. Ellen was eager to make a trip into the high country for a look at the white stallion. Pedro's shy-ness vanished when he talked about the horse. He be-came eloquent, his words coming so fast it was hard to keep up with him.

"But the first horse I want to see on the range is Golden Boy," Ellen said when Pedro stopped to catch his breath.

"We'll ride to the upper range tomorrow morning," Charlie promised.

After supper that night Ellen and Charlie sat on the front porch. Pedro and Shag had disappeared in the direction of the barn. Ellen leaned back and looked up at the evening star blazing above the highest peak of Bear Mountain.

"Pedro couldn't have done anything bad, but he's scared of something," she remarked thoughtfully.

"I think he plans to ride to Mexico if we can catch and tame the white stallion," Charlie said. He did not add that planning to cross the border made it look as though Pedro was running away from the law.

"Is that his home?" Ellen asked.

"I think he was born there," Charlie answered. "But I do not think he lived there very long."

They were both silent for a long time, each thinking about Pedro and wondering about him. Charlie finally pushed aside the thought that Pedro was running away from the law. A kid like Pedro could not be in bad trouble. If he was in trouble, he was the sort of kid who would face up to it.

They went indoors before ten o'clock and parted in the living room. Ellen went to her room and Charlie to his. When Pedro came in two hours later, Charlie was only dimly aware of it.

The next morning the boys caught a big roan gelding for Pedro to ride. Grandby had given the boy his pick of the extra saddle stock kept at the ranch. Diamond had always been Ellen's horse when she was visiting the ranch. With unerring horse sense Pedro picked a big and powerful horse that showed signs

of being high-strung and temperamental. Charlie
grinned as Pedro walked into the corral and dropped
his rope on the roan, apparently without even looking
at the other horses. Charlie knew that his father had
had his eye on the big saddler as a second-string horse
for himself.

"Has he a name?" Pedro asked as Charlie bridled
the roan and led him to the corral gate.

"We call him Casey Jones because he's really a free
wheeler when he gets going. He's a very good rope
horse. Shorty spent a lot of time training him."

"He is a horse with heart," Pedro said. "He will do
anything I ask of him."

Charlie grinned. "We call it bottom."

Pedro nodded gravely. "It is the same."

The boys saddled Diamond and their own horses.
As usual, Charlie was riding Trey Spot. He liked her,
in spite of her light weight. She was fast and she and
Charlie understood each other.

Shag was greatly excited. He made friends with
Ellen at once and stayed close to her side until she
mounted. At first she was a little afraid of the big
wolf dog, but Shag dispelled her fears by sitting up
and extending a big paw to her.

"He has a crippled foot," she said as she took the
paw and gravely shook it.

"It does not bother him," Pedro assured her.

On the ride up to the high benches Ellen was eager
and impatient. Mountain daisies spread fields of gold
over the slopes, and in the shaded spots blue-belled
columbine grew in clumps. A refreshing mountain
shower caught them as they were crossing the first

bench above Roaring River, and they made a wild dash for cover in a heavy stand of hemlocks.

When they came to the park where Golden Boy was watching over the ranch mares, Ellen changed horses with Charlie. She rode Trey Spot up to Golden Boy and managed to tempt him with some sugar lumps she had brought with her. Golden Boy was more nervous and alert than he had been for a long time. He broke away from Trey Spot and Ellen and circled his charges, stopping often to test the air and to send his call ringing down the slope. He seemed to be hurling a challenge at some unseen rival. Ellen joined the boys and changed back to Diamond.

"He's the most beautiful horse in the whole world," she said, her eyes shining.

Pedro smiled. "You have not seen the white stallion."

"Golden Boy is my first love," Ellen said stanchly. "Nothing can change that."

Charlie checked the horse herd and found none missing. The white stallion had not been able to stage another successful raid, probably because Golden Boy was now on the alert and watching for him.

Pedro had the hide-out of the white stallion located and an hour's ride brought them to it. The boys checked the wind and they made a careful approach. When they were as close as Charlie felt they should attempt, he handed Ellen his field glasses.

"We don't want to stampede them," he explained.

From the vantage of a high ridge they looked down upon the feed grounds of the white stallion. Charlie chuckled as he saw that the big fellow had increased his herd to seven mares. He wondered where the stallion had found them. They probably carried brands from other ranches.

"Where is he?" Ellen asked eagerly. "I can see mares but no stallion."

"On high ground between the two big spruce trees at the upper end of the park," Pedro said, and pointed to a low ridge above the meadow where the mares were feeding. Ellen trained the glasses on the spot and an excited gasp escaped her. She looked for a long time before she lowered the glasses.

"He is beautiful, but he looks savage." There was doubt in her voice. "Do you think you can tame him?"

"I can break him," Pedro said confidently.

Charlie laughed. Pedro reminded him of a banty rooster squaring off to tackle a big Plymouth Rock. He couldn't weigh over a hundred and ten pounds, yet he was confident he could tame the great brute on the ridge below. Well, he'd have help, Charlie thought. Shorty would be on hand and no horse ever walked that Shorty couldn't handle. It would be a big show with plenty of fireworks, but in the end the white stallion would be gentled or else given up as an outlaw.

They ate lunch in a pine grove. Charlie insisted that they rest an hour because Ellen had not been in a saddle for a long time. She refused to complain, but he knew her muscles must be sore, and he suspected that she might have developed a few blisters. Pedro lay on his back in the grass. He had been silent for almost an hour, listening to the talk but saying nothing. Shag sensed his master's mood and lay close to him with his head on his paws, his eyes on Pedro constantly.

Charlie held their pace to a slow trot on the way back to the ranch. Diamond rode very smoothly at such a pace. They reached home an hour before sunset. Ellen sighed as she slid from her saddle.

"It's been a wonderful day." She smiled up at Charlie. "I'm hungry as a bear, and I'll be in bed before it gets dark. A hot bath for my aches, cold cream for my sunburn, then I'll just pass out."

"Run along to the house. Pedro and I will take care of the horses," Charlie said.

Ellen did not need any urging. She walked slowly up the path, swinging her hat and humming softly to herself.

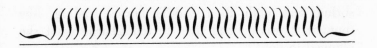

5. The Law

CHARLIE, ELLEN, AND PEDRO went to work on the trap. Supplies were loaded into a trail wagon. Pedro suggested that he and Shag camp near the site of the trap. He argued that by not having to ride back to the ranch every evening and out in the morning he would save a lot of time. Charlie could ride in with Ellen every night, but there was no reason why Pedro should not camp. The whole arrangement was reasonable, but it bothered Charlie. He noticed that Pedro was more at ease when he was away from the ranch.

It took a full day to drive the trail wagon into the high country. Camp had to be built several miles from the trap site, so as not to arouse the suspicion of the white stallion. Ellen realized that making the trip to the ranch every night would waste a lot of time for Charlie. She was riding beside him on the wagon's spring seat with their saddle horses trailing. She thought it was a good time to tell Charlie what she planned to do.

"I'll ride in alone and let you camp with Pedro," she offered.

Charlie flicked a fly off the fat rump of one of the work horses with the loose end of a line. "No," he said firmly. "But if you can stand it, we'll start from the ranch at four in the morning and ride back after dark."

"But I'm practically an old-timer. I know the trails," Ellen protested.

Charlie grinned at her. Twice before she had gotten herself into scrapes when he had let her ride alone or when she had been forced to ride in without him. He didn't have a very high regard for her trail sense.

"I want to do it that way," he argued. "It will be fun. We have to set up the trap in a few days, so it won't be any hardship."

Ellen smiled at him. "You win."

The trap was to be built in a small canyon at a spot where its walls widened. The canyon was a dry creek which led down to a deeper canyon. The whole setup formed a natural escape route from the benches above. Once the trap was built, it would be a matter of waiting until the white stallion and his mares were in the right position, so that when they were stampeded, they would charge down the little canyon, heading for the safety of the wild gorge below. Care would have to be taken that the big leader was not disturbed until the trap was ready.

Aspen poles were cut on a slope below the trap and

hauled to the site. Pedro and Shag set up camp beside a small stream. The camp was used as headquarters. To add to the day's outing, Ellen and Charlie had breakfast and supper with Pedro as well as lunch. Ellen elected herself camp cook, eliciting only feeble objections from the boys. The first day was a busy one, but everything was ready before darkness settled. Pedro would start cutting aspen poles the next morning.

Ellen and Charlie rode back to the ranch that night under the stars, tired but happy. Trey Spot was glad to have Charlie in the saddle. She had trailed along behind the wagon in a welter of dust. Diamond was irritated and kept blowing and snorting. The dust had really bothered him.

They had coffee in the kitchen after they cared for their horses. Ann joined them for a cup. It was clear that she had something on her mind, and she got to the point at once.

"I need an outing," she said. "I'll join you folks in camp, then you won't have to make the long ride back to the ranch every evening."

Charlie thought of his father. Grandby never let Ann ride unless he was along to make sure she held her horse to a walk. Ann noticed his hesitation. She smiled at him.

"I told your father what I am going to do," she explained. "I am sure he can trust me to be very careful."

"It will be wonderful having you," Ellen said impulsively.

"It will," Charlie agreed. He was remembering the

times when as a small boy he had gone for overnight trips into the mountains with his mother, camping beside streams, dashing madly across meadows, riding far and hard all day. It was Ann who had taught him most of what he knew about wood lore and horsemanship.

"I have the extra things laid out. Mrs. Garrity helped me get my camping outfit packed. It will all go on two pack horses."

Ann laughed eagerly. She was more excited than Charlie had seen her for a long time. He was worried, but he concealed it with a wide grin.

Grandby came in and poured himself coffee. He sat down beside his wife. It was easy to tell that he was worried, too. Ellen tried to assure him.

"We'll take good care of Ann," she said.

"You'll be a long way from the ranch," Grandby protested.

"I haven't felt a twinge for ages," Ann argued. "This is just what I need."

Grandby shrugged his shoulders helplessly. "With Charlie off on a horse hunt I won't be able to go with you." He frowned into his cup.

"You can ride up and spend all day Sunday with us," Ann suggested.

"I'll do that. I may even ride up Saturday afternoon." Grandby smiled. He knew he couldn't change her mind. When Ann had her heart attack, Grandby had promised himself that he would never let her ride again without him. Ann had been so untamed and wild, given to impulsive actions that were very often close to foolhardy.

"I'll cook up a special campfire mulligan for Sunday," Ann promised.

The next morning Ann was up before anyone, except Mrs. Garrity. The cook, as always, was determined that Ann should not get a chance to overexert herself. She followed her around the house and down to the corrals where Charlie was lashing on the packs.

At breakfast Tex was silent as usual, but Shorty was loud in his lamentations because he wasn't going to be in on the trap building.

"I haven't even seen the hoss yet," he said sadly.

"You can ride up Sunday," Charlie suggested.

"I sure will," Shorty said. "You kids are probably making a lot of mistakes."

For the first time in days Tex smiled. Grandby slapped Shorty on the shoulder.

"You'll be in on the drive and it will be up to you to take most of the starch out of that horse once we catch him," he said.

"You'll have Pedro to contend with," Charlie warned.

When they got under way, Charlie was careful to hold the pace to a fast walk. His mother was irked but curbed her impatience. Just being astride Diamond and headed for the high country was enough to make her spirits soar. She felt wonderful and was sure she was as strong as she had ever been. She meant to prove it before the trip was over.

They reached the camp late that afternoon. Pedro was away with the team and the trail wagon. Charlie noticed that Casey Jones was not picketed in the meadow below, but he did not look for the horse, even though Pedro's saddle lay beside his bedroll. He had to unpack the horses and make sure that his mother did not pitch in and help. Ann perched on a rock and supervised the setting up of a small tent and the rebuilding of the fire pit. Pedro and Charlie had merely rolled two flat rocks close together to have a place to set pots.

"We'll have ham and beans and lots of coffee for supper," she announced happily.

Charlie grinned broadly. His mother was already hedging. At home she limited herself to one cup of coffee in the morning and one in the evening. But he did not argue. Ann was so happy he did not want to spoil her fun.

Toward evening Pedro drove in with a load of aspen poles. He had Casey Jones in work harness beside a fat gelding. Casey Jones was not taking kindly to the arrangement, but it was clear that he had resigned himself to the indignity. Pedro jumped from the wagon. He smiled broadly when he saw Ann Carter.

"It is so good to have you with us, Mrs. Carter." He bowed low, sweeping off his battered Stetson.

"What happened to the work mare?" Charlie asked. The moment the words were out of his mouth he knew the answer, and laughed.

"She is now a part of the white stallion's harem." Pedro smiled and his eyes twinkled. "He stole her last night."

"How did you ever manage to get Casey Jones into work harness?" Charlie asked.

"I explained matters to him," Pedro said seriously.

"He was deeply insulted, but as my friend, he agreed to work, though he shows his temper at times."

Casey Jones rolled the white of an eye at Pedro and snorted. Pedro patted his neck. "I will quickly remove the harness so you can roll," he said soothingly.

Charlie helped unharness, water, and picket the team. He decided to take extra precautions to make sure that the white stallion did not make off with Trey Spot during the night. The big fellow not only knew the camp was there, but he was showing his contempt for the campers by raiding their horse herd.

Ann and Ellen had ham and beans and coffee ready when the boys returned from picketing the horses. Tin plates and tin cups were filled. As they ate, Pedro kept watching Charlie's mother. After he had finished his second cup of coffee, he spoke to her.

"It would be an honor to have you name the white stallion. He must have a name."

Ann was pleased. "If you will show him to me tomorrow, I'll try to think of a name for him."

"I will show you," Pedro agreed eagerly.

Charlie and Ellen wandered off for a walk through the gathering dusk. Pedro and Ann sat beside the campfire. Charlie had an idea that if Pedro wanted to confide in anyone, it would be his mother. When they returned, Ann was in the tent and Pedro was in his bedroll. Charlie said good night to Ellen. He sat for a time listening to the night sounds. The high country was different at night. Hundreds of small and big dwellers were abroad, seeking food, playing, or courting. Field mice scurried about the fire pit seeking crumbs; a stone rattled close above camp hinting at the presence of a curious coyote or bobcat. Shag stirred in his sleep and growled but did not lift his head. It was great to be alive and part of a country like this, Charlie decided as he stripped off his boots and got ready for bed.

The next morning Pedro and Ann started out before the sun was up. They were back by ten o'clock. Ann was very enthusiastic about the white stallion.

"He's a beauty," she said. "But we must never let him meet Golden Boy."

"Did you name him?" Ellen asked.

"I called him Prince." Ann smiled. "He has an air of royalty about him." She laughed.

"The name fits him well," Pedro said.

"He's a prince," Ellen agreed. "Like the princes of the barbarian tribes."

"Fits him," Charlie said.

The boys brought in the fat work horse and Casey Jones. They harnessed the team and drove down to the trap, where they went to work with post augers and set the poles for the corral. After they had set all the cut poles, they drove to the aspen grove for another load.

It was late afternoon before Charlie and Pedro got enough poles cut to make a load. They drove to the camp. Charlie was surprised to see Grandby's saddle horse feeding close to camp with two other Bar L saddle horses. Charlie got down from the wagon. Pedro joined him but did not move forward. Grandby arose from the shade of a tree. With him were Sheriff Colby and a stranger who looked familiar to Charlie.

"Hello, Charlie," Colby said.

"Hello, Sheriff," Charlie answered. He had a sick feeling at the pit of his stomach. He had suddenly remembered where he had seen the stranger and under what circumstances. He was the man who had stood listening while Charlie was talking to Mike in the poolroom.

The sheriff turned to the tall man. "Is that the boy?" He jerked a thumb toward Pedro.

"That's him, Pedro Martinez, the one that killed my partner, Dillon."

The sheriff saw that Charlie was staring at the tall stranger. He gruffly introduced the man.

"Mitch Seller. He's the state witness."

Charlie stepped close to Sheriff Colby, hot anger swelling inside him. "I don't believe it," he said flatly. "This man is lying."

"That's for a jury to decide." The sheriff looked straight at Grandby. "I've delayed a few days in coming out here. Figured you'd bring the boy in. You must have been wondering about him." He turned to face Pedro. "You have to come along with me, son."

Pedro stumbled as he stepped forward. He seemed numb. Charlie reached out and steadied him. Pedro looked up into Charlie's face. In answer to the question in Charlie's eyes, he said:

"I did not kill him."

"I believe you," Charlie said, his voice rough with anger.

"He shot him, all right." Seller took a step toward Pedro. "He's a dirty Mex. I warned Dillon against trusting him."

Charlie whirled and stepped in fast. Before Sheriff Colby or Grandby could move, Charlie was toe to toe with Seller. His right fist shot out, catching the tall man on the chin. Seller staggered back and sat down with a thud. Charlie stood over him, his eyes blazing.

"You filthy scum," he snarled.

Sheriff Colby caught Charlie by the arm and spun him around. Grandby closed in fast. Ann and Ellen stood at the tent flap, watching. Ellen was clutching Ann's hand. Sheriff Colby's voice was smooth and controlled.

"Keep your shirt on, Charlie. I'll take care of the state witness. There'll be no more rough talk." He gave Seller a cold stare. Seller got to his feet and backed away.

Charlie looked toward the tent. There were tears in Ellen's eyes, but his mother was dry-eyed and her head was up. She walked to Pedro's side and slipped an arm around the boy.

"We know you are innocent, Pedro," she said gently. "We'll help you prove it."

"I'll drive to town tomorrow," Grandby said grimly. "My wife expresses my sentiments. We owe this boy a great deal. I'll see to it that he isn't railroaded for something he did not do."

Pedro looked into the faces of his friends and some of the fear left his eyes. His mouth moved, but no words came.

"No one is going to get railroaded while I'm sheriff of this county," Colby said sharply.

"I'll ride in with you," Charlie offered.

Pedro straightened and his chin came up. "I want you to stay and trap Prince."

"The stallion can wait," Charlie told him grimly. He was still fighting mad.

"It might be best if we all rode in," Grandby suggested. "We can leave the wagon here, and the camp

outfit. Shorty can bring it in." He looked at Casey
Jones and almost smiled. "Casey Jones will like a saddle better than that harness."

Seller grumbled, but not very loudly, and he stayed
away from Charlie. The camp was put in order and
Casey Jones and the other horses were saddled. It was
a silent group that mounted and rode away from the
camp.

Charlie rode beside his father. There were a lot of
questions he wanted answered. Being an old friend
of the sheriff, Grandby would have learned all the
facts known to the law.

"How bad is it?" Charlie asked his father when they
had dropped behind the others.

"Quite bad," Grandby said. "Pedro worked with
Seller and Dillon rounding up wild horses in the south
end of the county. That's pretty rough and isolated
country—no ranches there, only a few high-line
camps. Pedro had an argument with Dillon over
money from the sale of horses. Dillon was killed with
Pedro's six-gun, and the money is missing. Seller
swears that he came to the cabin and found Pedro
there with the dead man."

"This is all Seller's story?" Charlie asked.

"Seller says the boy threatened him. He took the
gun from him, but Pedro managed to get away and
run into the woods." Grandby frowned.

"Has Seller an alibi?" Charlie asked hopefully. For
his money, Seller was the killer.

"Two cowboys will swear that Seller was playing
poker with them at their high-line camp all that day,"
Grandby answered.

"His story is full of holes," Charlie said hotly. "If Seller had taken the gun away from Pedro, and the kid made a break for it, Seller would have shot him. He's that kind of man."

"It's a weak alibi, I agree." Grandby shook his head. "We'll get Pedro's side of the story when Colby questions him."

"I'd like to hear it," Charlie said.

"I might talk Colby into questioning him in my office. I can suggest that he would talk more freely with you and me on hand." Grandby glanced up to where the sheriff was riding beside Pedro.

Ellen dropped back and Charlie joined her. He hoped that his father could talk the sheriff into questioning the boy before taking him to jail. They both watched the hunched-over figure riding between Colby and Seller. Pedro looked pitifully small and frail. Ellen spoke in a tight voice.

"No one could believe he shot a man."

"I'm going to dig up evidence that will clear him," Charlie said, anger edging his voice. "Before I'm through, I'll have the goods on that tramp Seller." His plans for trapping the white stallion were forgotten, along with his worry about Golden Boy and the mares. His eyes dropped to Shag, who was trotting close to Casey Jones's heels. The dog appeared as dejected as his master.

"We'll have to keep Shag at the ranch," he said. "When I'm away, you can keep an eye on him. I don't trust Tex when it comes to a dog."

"I'll take care of Shag, and we have to trap that white stallion."

Charlie glanced at Ellen. He suddenly realized that she was being the practical one. She was facing reality, meeting all the problems instead of going off the deep end.

"You're right," he agreed. "But the main thing is to clear Pedro."

"You'll clear him, because he's innocent." It was as simple as that to Ellen.

Charlie felt pretty low. If his father was worried, that meant the case looked bad for Pedro. But he meant to do everything he could to help.

"The first thing I'm going to do is to check Seller's alibi," Charlie said.

"But the sheriff has done that," Ellen said doubtfully.

"I'll do it again."

"I guess we can't pass up any chance," Ellen admitted.

They had lagged far behind. The rest of the party was at the house when they arrived at the corrals. Charlie hurriedly cared for their horses, and then they almost ran up the path. Charlie was afraid that he would miss part of Pedro's story.

As they passed the bunkhouse, they saw that Tex and Shorty were entertaining Seller. He did not seem to be enjoying it. Charlie had an idea Grandby had asked them to make sure Seller wasn't in on the questioning.

In the house they found Colby and Pedro in the front room with Grandby. Ann was absent and Charlie guessed she had gone upstairs in order to leave the men alone. The sheriff nodded to Charlie. Ellen went upstairs to join Ann.

"Pedro wants to tell his story. I'm letting him tell it here. That's my right, as I see it." He glanced at Grandby, then turned to Pedro. "Go ahead, son."

"Begin at the beginning," Grandby urged. "How you met these men and what sort of understanding you had with them."

Sheriff Colby nodded his approval.

"Shag and I were going to try to catch a few head by ourselves. We had a herd located." Pedro looked the sheriff in the eye. "I told Dillon about it and he said we'd split three ways. He and his partner would help me. I had a horse of my own then." Pedro looked at the sheriff as though trying to be sure he was being believed.

"Go on, son," the sheriff said.

"They came to the abandoned trapper's cabin where I was camped, and stayed. We caught twenty horses. Dillon sold them and he sold my horse with them." Pedro turned to Charlie. "So I had a right to take one of their horses. I took a very old one."

The sheriff nodded. "Tell us about your trouble with Dillon over the money."

"He did not give me a third. I did not get any money." An angry flush spread over the boy's face. "I did not even get a horse. I scouted on foot with Shag."

"Did you threaten to shoot Dillon?" Colby asked.

"No," Pedro said slowly. "I had no gun."

"But it was your gun that killed Dillon." The sheriff pulled a pipe out of his pocket and started filling it.

"It was my gun, but it had been taken days before Dillon was shot with it. I do not know who took it. I could not find it when I looked for it." Pedro frowned.

"What happened the day Dillon was shot?" Sheriff Colby had his pipe going smoothly.

"I came in late. I do not know the time, because I have no watch. I opened the cabin door and Dillon was lying on the floor. My gun was beside him. I went in and knelt down. I thought he was dead, because there was blood, but I had to be sure. If he was alive, I could help him." Pedro looked at Charlie.

"Go ahead," Charlie urged.

Pedro shook his head. "He was dead. I picked up my gun. Whoever had stolen it had shot Dillon. Seller came in when I had my back to the door. He pinned my arms and took the gun."

"Then what happened?" the sheriff asked.

"He said he knew I had killed Dillon. He said he had been playing cards with two cowboys, and they would swear it was the truth. I would be electrocuted. He said he was taking me in to the sheriff." Pedro paused and something that was almost a smile touched his lips. "Shag never liked Seller. He knew from my voice that there was trouble. He leaped at Seller and got him by the wrist, the hand with the gun." Pedro's voice rose as he remembered. "Seller fired and kept on firing until the gun was empty. That was when Shag and I escaped. Without a loaded gun, he was afraid of Shag."

"Why didn't Shag finish him?" the sheriff asked.

"I called him off. Shag was going for his throat."

Pedro looked down at his hands, then up at the sheriff. "That is all. I got my saddle and took one of their horses. Seller had no more cartridges. I had them in my bedroll. We left." He sat for a long minute thinking, then went on. "I was sure the law would kill me. Seller would swear, and the cowboys would swear, I had told Dillon I'd get even."

"Did you search the cabin for the money? A third of it was yours." The sheriff smiled at Pedro.

Pedro shook his head. "I was only in the cabin a few minutes. I did not look anywhere but at the body and at my gun. After I left the cabin, I caught a horse, saddled it, and rode away. The next day I met Charlie Carter. I wouldn't have let him see me if he hadn't been in trouble."

"A straightforward story and one that anyone should believe," Grandby commented.

"I have been framed," Pedro said. "Seller is lying."

"Could be," the sheriff said. "Now we'd better get into my car and head for town."

"Don't you believe him?" Charlie asked angrily.

"I've checked those cowboys and I've checked Seller's story." Sheriff Colby regarded Charlie somberly. "And I'll check Pedro's story. I'd say right now that it's what a jury believes that will count."

Charlie leaned forward. "Why would Seller want to frame you, Pedro?"

"Seller hated Dillon, but he was afraid of him. I heard Dillon tell a horse buyer that if he was ever found shot in the back, the law better start working on Seller."

"Remember the name of that horse buyer?" the sheriff asked.

"No." Pedro shook his head. "I only saw him once. I never talked to him. Seller and I were standing back of the buyer's trail wagon."

"Did Seller hear what Dillon said?" Grandby asked.

"Yes. He was right beside me."

"There—you have a clear picture, Sheriff," Charlie said triumphantly.

"Not too clear," Colby answered. "We don't know who the horse buyer was."

"You know where this buyer was from?" Charlie asked.

Pedro shook his head.

"Could be from any of a hundred places; could be one of those buyers who are always on the move," Colby said.

"You can ask Seller," Charlie suggested.

"I'll ask Seller." Colby was frowning deeply.

Ellen and Ann came down to the living room and walked to the sheriff's car with the men. Pedro got into the car. He looked out at his friends and forced a smile. Seller came stamping up from the bunkhouse. He got into the car and slammed the door. Grandby stepped close and spoke to Pedro.

"I'll see you tomorrow. My lawyer will be with me. We'll get to the bottom of this." He gave Seller a cold, level look. Seller scowled at Grandby.

"The D.A. will hear about the secret session you put on with the sheriff," he said.

Sheriff Colby dropped the car into gear and drove

away. Ellen and Charlie led the way back to the house. In the living room Grandby faced his son.

"We have to decide what to do about that wild stallion. I can send Tex up there to rid the range of him, or we can go ahead and trap him. But he can't be left running loose. If he gets the best of Golden Boy, he'll make off with the mares."

"We'll trap him," Charlie said. "Pedro would never forgive us if we shot him."

"That means you should be on the job up there. You can leave matters in town to me." Grandby was watching Charlie closely.

"There are some things I have to find out for myself," Charlie said stubbornly. "I'll have to let the trapping go for a few days."

Grandby shrugged his shoulders. He turned and went into his office. Charlie knew he had angered his father, but he had a feeling that he was the only one who really realized the spot Pedro was in. He had to crack Seller's alibi.

6. No Quarter Asked

CHARLIE STRAPPED a blanket roll and a supply of grub to the back of his saddle. He had set his alarm for four o'clock, and no one was awake when he left the house. He hadn't seen his father after Grandby had entered his office the night before, and he had not confided in his mother or Ellen. This was a quest he had to make, even though the others might think it foolish and a loss of time in building the horse trap. Grandby and Ann would drive to town in the car. Where Charlie was going only a horse could go.

The south end of the county lay beyond a high divide. On the far slope he would find Ike Dowd and Pete Lester, the two hands who were giving Seller his alibi. The trip would take him into wild country where there were no ranches. The high-line camp he sought was operated by the KT ranch as a border station where they kept two drift-fence riders.

Charlie knew that Ellen planned to take Shag and ride up to the camp in the breaks. Charlie had almost given up his trip when he thought of her making the long ride alone, but she had argued that her being up there might prevent trouble between the rivals. She had promised him that she would start home by mid-afternoon, and that she would not interfere if there was a fight. Shorty planned to go up and check on the herd if possible. With Grandby gone, this did not seem likely.

While plans were being changed down at the ranch, Golden Boy was standing guard over his herd. He had been watchful during the night and had grazed very little. Now that dawn was breaking, he relaxed and started cropping the tall grass eagerly. The mares were below him in a meadow well away from the timber. At intervals the big stallion lifted his head and tested the air, turning slowly to stare around the dark circle of spruce and pines which surrounded the park.

His first warning of trouble came when he spotted a white form moving through the trees on his right and below him. He was instantly alert, keyed to action. Whirling, he sent a loud warning call ringing down across the meadow. The mares lifted their heads and stared at him. They were not wild mares, and took alarm slowly. Several of them started moving toward the center of the meadow. The four racing mares shook their heads eagerly. They were always ready for a mad run.

When the white stallion trotted out of the woods,

Golden Boy broke into a gallop and charged down upon his mares. The white challenger screamed savagely, and Golden Boy answered the scream as he cut across the meadow to intercept the invader. He ran with powerful strides, his legs churning like pistons. The white stallion floated along, pacing smoothly, seeming to run with effortless ease. He swerved a little to meet the charge of the big palomino.

The challenger had hoped to make off with part of the herd before Golden Boy could reach them. He could not do this, so he accepted the gage of battle. He had to defeat the golden horse charging toward him with teeth bared and hoofs lashing. He was young and inexperienced, but there was no fear in him, only a savage eagerness to meet and smash his foe.

Golden Boy was filled with a similar rage which left no room for caution or fear. He made no attempt at a shifty advance which might have thrown his adversary off balance; instead, he met the white stallion head on, reaching for his neck with bared teeth, and lashing at his chest with huge hoofs. They came together with staggering impact. Golden Boy's teeth found flesh and sank deep. He ripped a great gash in the neck of the white stallion as the two staggered apart, shaken by the meeting of their two heavy bodies. The pain from the wound and the smell of blood added to the wrath of the challenger.

For a moment they faced each other and screamed wildly, then they both reared up and lashed out like boxers. The blows landed. The weight of the two horses was so nearly the same that there was little advantage in a charging attack. Neither horse could hurl the other from his feet. But they did charge, and came together in a crushing collision. They broke apart and, as though by common consent, whirled and placed distance between them before charging again. This time the white stallion gave ground. Golden Boy had been grain-hardened before being turned loose on the range. Charlie had seen to it that he had the extra hardness that grain gives over straight grass. Golden Boy was quick to follow up his advantage. He lunged forward and smashed at the neck and shoulders of the challenger. The white stallion was off balance now, unable to strike back with power. He was pounded back toward the steep bank of an arroyo.

Eagerly Golden Boy lunged to finish his rival. The white stallion leaped sidewise in a desperate attempt to escape the pounding hoofs. As he leaped, he lashed out with his hind feet. His hoofs struck Golden Boy's shoulder and found bone under the hard layer of muscles. Searing pain shot through the big palomino. He whirled and struck out blindly. His hoofs found the head and neck of the white stallion. The challenger had made a costly mistake when he lowered his head to lash out. Golden Boy's blows had the effect of a prize fighter's one-two punch to the chin of an opponent. The white stallion went to his knees, his legs gone rubbery and weak. In a split second Golden Boy was on him, biting and smashing. The challenger went down. He fell at the edge of the arroyo and rolled over the bank. Kicking and struggling, he tumbled to the bottom of the arroyo. Luck was with him. Had he been on level ground, Golden Boy would have ended his career within a few minutes.

The big palomino stood at the top of the bank and sent a triumphant cry ringing after his defeated opponent. But he did not try to follow. His leg was numb and refused to move when he started forward. He ignored the pain, but the leg refused to obey his bidding.

At the bottom of the arroyo the white stallion scrambled to his feet. He was still groggy from the head blows, and his vision was foggy. For the moment, all the fight was out of him. He shook his head slowly and started down the bed of the arroyo. Before he had gone a hundred yards, his head started to clear, but he kept on going. The rage to kill had cooled. Like any wounded wild animal he wanted to get away and lick his bruises. He would return and fight again, after he had recovered from the beating he had taken. Also, instinct told him that he had better get back to his mares before they scattered and deserted him. He had already learned that they were fickle creatures, paying him homage only when he was on hand to demand it.

Golden Boy turned slowly away from the arroyo. He tried to gallop back to his herd, but the best he could manage was a slow trot, a three-legged gait with one foreleg dragging uselessly. His shoulder and right leg had started to swell. Unknowing, the white stallion was retreating when victory would have been easy and sure. Golden Boy moved in close to the mares. He threatened a young filly who started to-

Golden Boy sounded a triumphant cry

ward the woods, and the sight of his bared teeth and angry cry made her hurry back to join the mares. He had only the fear that they had of him to hold them together, the memory of his quick chastisement. Angrily Golden Boy limped around the herd, dragging his helpless leg, his eyes watchful for the return of the white stallion.

When Ellen and Shag arrived an hour before noon, Golden Boy was standing on high ground. His swollen leg had forced him to stop circling the herd and stand propped on three legs. He was in no mood to welcome a visitor. As Ellen rode toward him on Diamond, he laid back his ears and shook his head threateningly. Ellen halted Diamond and sat looking at the stallion. He was bloody, and his swollen shoulder gave him an odd lopsided look. When she brought Diamond closer, Golden Boy started to move. His pain-racked movements brought a cry from Ellen. Shag trotted close to the stallion and sniffed the dried blood. He whined and turned back toward Ellen.

"I got here too late," Ellen said to herself bitterly.

Ellen felt she should get Golden Boy down to the ranch where Shorty could doctor him. But she had no saddle rope, so she decided to drive him ahead of Diamond. Golden Boy refused to be driven; he would not leave the herd. He faced Diamond and showed signs of being willing to fight. Diamond wanted no part of a fight with the stallion. Ellen wasn't sure she could drive the herd to the ranch. But she felt Golden Boy would go along if she could drive the mares down to the valley.

She finally decided to find out what had happened

to Prince. Grandby might not want the mares brought in. Prince might no longer be a menace. She located the spot where the white stallion had gone over the bank into the arroyo. Diamond made the descent to the dry stream bed below. Shag picked up the stallion's trail and Ellen followed the dog. She was on the trail an hour before she sighted Prince. From a hemlock grove she watched the stallion and his mares. The mares were feeding peacefully, but Prince was pacing about nervously, head up, nostrils flaring. Ellen realized at once that he had not suffered any great injury. His head and neck were stained with dried blood—that could be seen even at a distance— but he appeared to be in high spirits.

Ellen decided the best thing to do was to stampede the stallion and his herd. If she gave Prince a bad scare, he might run far into the breaks; he might even decide to leave the range and cross the mountains. Panic took hold of her as she watched the white stallion. He looked savage and powerful. What if he attacked instead of running? Shag sat looking up at her eagerly. He had trailed the white horse; now he wanted to know what she wished him to do. Ellen pulled off her hat. Taking a deep breath, she headed Diamond into the open. She called to Shag,

"Sick them, Shag; chase them!"

She had no idea of how to say it so that the dog would understand. Shag leaped ahead. He did not know what she wanted but had an idea that she was telling him to round up the horses.

When she broke into the open meadow, Ellen shouted as loudly as she could and waved her hat. She spurred Diamond to his top speed. Shag raced ahead, barking wildly. Instantly Prince sounded an alarm and charged down upon his mares. They bunched quickly and whirled for flight. Prince sent them thundering toward a steep bank which dropped off into a small canyon. Ellen realized that the white stallion was stampeding his herd down a trail that would take them past the spot where the trap should have been waiting. If things had worked out right, this could

have been the run that ended in the capture of Prince.

Shag had closed up on the flying horses and was trying to turn them back. The white stallion saw the dog and whirled. To him, Shag was a wolf attacking his mares. He charged at Shag and tried to smash him into the ground. Shag dodged and ducked the big hoofs. He decided to treat Prince the same way he would an angry bull. As the hoofs flashed past him, he leaped high and reached for the muzzle of the big horse. He got a solid hold and hung on. Prince screamed in fury and swung his powerful neck. Shag's hold loosened and he was tossed high into the air. He landed with a jolt that shook the wind out of him. Prince leaped forward to stamp the prostrate dog. Diamond closed in at that moment. Ellen was using her spurs savagely to make the big gelding close with the white stallion. Forgotten was her fear; she had to save Shag.

Prince hesitated for a second in his attack on Shag. A human being on a horse was charging down on him. He caught man smell, and the screams of the rider filled him with panic. Man was the only animal he feared. Whirling, he plunged down the bank and fled on the heels of the mares. Ellen pulled up and started to dismount. But Shag was on his feet. He shook himself and snarled deeply, then he bounded down the steep bank and raced after the horses. In spite of herself Ellen laughed. She rode to the top of the bank and shouted to Shag, calling his name over and over. She didn't want him to catch up with Prince. She was sure that if she rode after the horses, Shag would have another try at the stallion. So she sat and waited. Fifteen minutes later Shag came loping back. He had decided that she did not want to round up the herd, because she had stopped chasing them.

Shag wagged his tail as he climbed the bank. He was fagged out, but he wanted to receive his reward from Ellen. He jumped up against her stirrup and placed his paws on the saddle skirt.

"Good boy," Ellen said, patting his head. "You're a mighty brave fellow." Then she added, "What are we going to do about Golden Boy?"

Shag whined eagerly and laid his head against her leg. He knew she was worried and wanted her to understand that he was ready to help her.

"I guess we better ride to the ranch and tell Shorty and Tex." She frowned. "I guess we better just tell Shorty. Tex might come up with his rifle. He's the boss when Grandby is away."

She rode back, past the park where the ranch mares were grazing. Golden Boy was standing where she had left him. Except for the swollen shoulder, he looked very much the invincible leader. But when he moved to face Diamond, his action was clumsy and slow. Ellen bit her lip and winked back tears. She knew enough about ranch practices to realize that if the stallion's shoulder bones were broken, he would have to be shot.

She rode down the mountain, letting Diamond set his own pace. It was a fast lope. Diamond was glad to put a lot of distance between himself and the two stallions. There was no one at the ranch when she arrived but Mrs. Garrity. Tex was expected back for supper, but Shorty had taken food and blankets when he left that morning. Mrs. Garrity did not expect him to return before the next evening.

"He wants to get the upper drift fence fixed so he can go after that white horse," Mrs. Garrity explained. "He won't rest until he gets his hands on that critter." She placed her ample palms on her hips and shook her head. "Imagine a grown man believing all that bosh about a horse. He'll probably have a ring spavin when they catch him."

"There's nothing wrong with Prince. He's a lot of horse," Ellen said, then added with a smile, "But he probably does have a sore nose right now."

Mrs. Garrity fussed with a pot of stew simmering on the stove. She dipped some stew out of the pot with a wooden spoon and frowned as she sampled it. With a deep sigh she set the spoon aside.

"I can't get that boy out of my mind. I keep thinking of him down there locked up in Colby's jail."

"He's innocent. Juries do not convict innocent people." Ellen tried to sound convincing.

"I've seen more than one innocent man framed in my time," Mrs. Garrity said grimly. "Right here in this county they sent Tom Caxton up for twenty years for a crime he never committed."

"Charlie and Grandby will find new evidence." Ellen forced a smile.

"They better." Mrs. Garrity's manner showed plainly that she held little hope for Pedro.

Ellen went into the living room. She paced the floor and finally halted at the open front door and stood looking out over the wide meadows. A fleeting form was moving across the upper cow pasture. It was Shag and he was running with the swinging strides of a wolf, heading toward the mouth of Roaring River Canyon. He's restless and out looking for Pedro, Ellen thought. For a moment she felt a stirring of uneasiness, but put it aside. Shag could be trusted even if he did run like a wolf.

Tex came in as Mrs. Garrity was putting supper on

the table. The three sat down to eat. Tex was silent for a while. Finally he looked across the table at Ellen.

"You were up on the horse range today?"

"Yes." Ellen did not add any information.

"Shorty is finishing the fence mending. We aim to get up to the breaks and work on that trap day after tomorrow." A hint of a smile touched the corners of Tex's wide mouth.

Ellen was too surprised to answer for a moment. Then she gave Tex a warm smile. "That will be wonderful," she said. "I'll ride along and help."

"It won't take long to throw up a tight corral." Tex applied himself to his stew and said no more about their plans to capture the white stallion.

Ellen was thinking that she had probably ruined their chances of catching Prince. She was also disturbed over what the men would do when they saw Golden Boy. But she decided not to confide in Tex. He might take drastic action. But she was pleased by the way Tex was acting. Under his tough exterior there was a warm heart.

She wondered if she had done the right thing in not confiding in Tex. She could have told Mrs. Garrity, but somehow she felt that until she had talked to Charlie or Ann, she should not tell anyone what had happened. She was confused, she admitted, and not sure what to do.

7. Alibi

CHARLIE FOLLOWED a little-used trail over the mountain. He had once hunted elk in this country and knew some of the landmarks. The KT high-line cabin was on Willow Creek. Charlie was sure that he could find it. He rode down into Willow Creek and followed it for two miles before sighting the small log cabin.

Two horses were feeding in a small pasture below the cabin. This was a good sign. He probably would find Dowd and Lester in the cabin. But when he stopped at the door and shouted, no one answered. He dismounted and stepped to the cabin door. When he opened it, he saw that the cabin was deserted. The place smelled musty and unused. There were a sheet-iron stove, a rough table with two benches beside it, and a packing-case cupboard. Two bunks stood along one wall. The blankets on the bunks were soiled and greasy. Charlie stepped into the room and stood beside the table. A thick coating of dust covered it. No one had used the table for a week or more. He wondered about the horses in the pasture and decided to check their brands.

When he stepped outside, he took a deep breath of the mountain air, clearing his nostrils of the musty smell inside the cabin. Heavy pack-rat odor followed him. He turned and closed the door. There was something very wrong about the setup. Charlie frowned as he tried to figure it out. He led Trey Spot down to the fence and checked the horses. They both carried the KT brand.

Charlie was convinced there was no point in waiting for the return of the fence riders. He had a hunch that he would find them in Cedar Bank. He wondered if Amos Jenkins, owner of the KT, knew that his drift-fence riders had deserted their job. He decided to call Amos when he got to a phone. The KT horses

could not stay in the small pasture much longer. There
was water, but the grass was limited. He could ride
around the mountain and reach Cedar Bank without
climbing back over the divide to Roaring River Valley.
Mounting, he sent Trey Spot down the creek at an
easy lope, a ground-devouring pace that she could
hold for hours without tiring.

It was midafternoon when Charlie rode into Cedar
Bank. He had pushed Trey Spot hard and she was
fagged. Riding to a stable, he turned her over to the
boy in charge, ordering a rub and an extra measure
of oats for her before he left the barn.

"She's a fine horse," the boy said as he jerked loose
the cinch strap.

"Tops," Charlie admitted.

Charlie headed for the hardware store and a phone.
After some delay he got Amos Jenkins on the phone
and told him about the horses.

"They must have pay coming," he said. "They'll
probably be riding by to pick it up. I'd appreciate it
if you'd call me when they show up."

"They won't show here," Amos said. "I advanced
them cash for outfits. They're ahead of me. But I
would like a word with those saddle tramps."

"So would I," Charlie said.

Leaving the hardware store, he walked up the street
to the poolroom. That seemed the most likely place
to find Dowd and Lester. He kept his eyes open for
the Bar L Buick, but did not see it. His father and
mother probably were on their way home.

The proprietor of the poolroom greeted Charlie when

he entered. He had just sold a cigar to a rancher. He propped his elbows on the glass case and leaned forward.

"Hear Colby picked up a killer out at the Bar L." It was clear that the proprietor was fishing for details.

Charlie held his temper in check. "The boy is no more a killer than you are," he said with feeling.

"Hear your father's going to bat for the kid." The proprietor was watching Charlie's face closely. Charlie gave him a level stare that made the man shift his gaze to a pair of cow hands at the end of the bar.

"We all are going to back him," Charlie said. He shifted his position so that he could see the loungers in the room. "I'm looking for a couple of hands named Dowd and Lester. Have they been in?"

"They're back at the card table, the two wearing black hats." The proprietor took a cigar from the case and looked at the perforated end before lighting it. "They got something to do with the kid's trial—witnesses, I guess."

Charlie nodded and moved away from the case. He walked into the back room and over to the card table, which stood near a window. Four men were playing draw poker. Charlie studied the two wearing battered black hats. He pretended to be watching the game, but his attention was fixed on the ex-fence riders. One was short and swarthy, with a pock-marked face. The other was thin, with big hands and a hatchet-sharp face. He had a pointed chin and a very long nose. Feeling Charlie's eyes on him, he looked up. For a space of almost a minute he stared at Charlie, then gave his attention to his cards. The chunky man did not look up, but Charlie knew he had been watching as closely as his pal.

"Raise you four," he said to the man across the table. His hand moved forward and dropped four white chips.

The man tossed his cards into the center of the table and got to his feet. He was a cow hand Charlie had met a number of times. As he turned away from the table, he grinned at Charlie.

"Slickers," he said in an amused voice. "Slickers palming an ace in a game for house drinks."

The thin man glared at the back of the cow hand, who was on his way to the door. The third man at the table got to his feet. He did not say anything, but his expression was far from the amused smile of the cowboy. Charlie sat down at the table.

"You Dowd and Lester?" he asked abruptly.

The chunky man said, "I'm Dowd." Lester scowled but said nothing.

"Have you quit the KT?" Charlie asked.

"Did a spell of fence riding. Got through," Dowd answered. "You looking for hands?"

"I'm Charlie Carter of the Bar L. I just wanted to ask you a few questions."

A wary look came into Dowd's eyes. Lester pulled a muslin tobacco sack and papers from his shirt pocket. He spilled tobacco into a paper and deftly rolled a cigarette. There was no expression on his face.

"You were playing poker in your cabin with Seller the day Dillon was killed, that right?" Charlie leaned back and watched Dowd's face.

"That's right. We played all day. Mitch left along

toward evening." Dowd frowned. "What's it to you?"

"I'm interested," Charlie said. "How far is it from the high-line cabin to Dillon's place?"

"Never been to his place. Mitch said it was about a mile." Dowd started gathering the cards into a pack.

"What time did Seller leave your cabin?" Charlie asked. He had a feeling he wasn't going to get anything out of the pair. They were wary and tough.

Dowd regarded him coldly. "We aren't talking until the trial," he said.

"Where you boys from?" Charlie asked. He had to keep at them; he was sure they could tell a lot that would help Pedro.

"That's none of your business, kid. Shove off." Lester spoke in a thin voice. He placed his big hands on the table and pushed his chair back. "I said, shove off." He started to get to his feet.

Charlie looked across the table at him and smiled. "Start something and you'll get yourself locked up in Colby's jail. That will mean he'll fingerprint you."

Dowd's chair scraped as he heaved himself to his feet. "Keep your shirt on, Pete!" he growled. He turned and looked down at Charlie. "Where we come from folks don't ask a lot of nosy questions."

Charlie did not move. He watched the two men gather up their chips and move away to the main room to cash them. He felt frustrated. He should have started a fight with Pete Lester. Colby might have taken them both in and fingerprinted them. He had a feeling they might have records. He decided he wasn't much of a detective.

Leaving the poolroom, Charlie walked five blocks

to the county courthouse. He went around to the back where the jail entrance opened on an alley. Colby was in his small office, seated at his desk.

"Hello, Charlie," he said, glancing up. "Want to see the boy?"

"Later." Charlie sat down beside the desk. Colby looked up and frowned. He spoke patiently.

"I've been over this case with the D.A. and with your father and with the defense attorney and with half the people in town. I reckon I have to go over what I've got with you."

"I'm interested in Dowd and Lester," Charlie said.

"So am I."

"I almost picked a fight with Lester." Charlie smiled. "I figured if you jailed us, you'd get a set of his fingerprints."

"I got both of their prints from beer glasses they used at the poolroom," Colby said grimly, "and I'm sending them around to sheriffs' offices and to the FBI."

"That pair just have to have records," Charlie said stubbornly.

"I even included some prints my deputy managed to snap. No reports so far." The sheriff picked up his cold pipe and turned it over slowly. "I've been on this a week. I've had time to check a good many angles."

"They're both lying," Charlie said flatly, then he asked about Seller. "Did you get the name of the horse buyer from Seller?"

Colby shook his head. "Seller says no horse buyer came to get the horses. He says Pedro made up the story about the horse buyer. Dillon delivered the horses to the buyer at a KT corral down the creek, according to Seller."

"An abandoned corral," Charlie said.

"Hasn't been used for two years." Colby chewed at the stem of his cold pipe. "Seller says neither he nor Pedro went with Dillon to deliver the horses."

"More lies," Charlie said bitterly.

"Could be," Colby answered. "Want to see the kid?"

Charlie got to his feet. "How's he taking it?" he asked.

"He's given up hope." Colby got slowly to his feet. He took a large key ring from a hook and turned toward a hall door.

The jail had only one cell. Pedro sat on a cot, staring at the floor. When Colby unlocked the door, he looked up. Charlie grinned at him.

"Hello, Pedro," he said, forcing a cheerful note into his voice.

Pedro gave him a wan smile. Colby closed the door and returned to his office. Charlie sat down on the cot beside Pedro.

"We're going to get you out of here," he said grimly.

"It's no use. Seller is lying and the two cow hands are backing him up." Pedro spoke in a low voice. "Your father got me a lawyer." He turned his head to face Charlie. "Do you know what the lawyer says I should do?"

"No." Charlie placed a hand on Pedro's arm.

"He wants me to plead guilty," Pedro said dully. "That way he says there won't be a trial, and I'll be

sent to reform school until I'm of age." Pedro's chin
came up and his voice stiffened. "But I'm not guilty.
If I plead guilty, I'll always be a criminal."

"Don't do it!" Charlie's voice was edged with anger.
"We'll get a break; we'll find the real murderer."

Pedro straightened his shoulders. "You're finishing
the trap?"

"We'll finish it and catch your horse," Charlie promised.

"Shag has given you no trouble?"

"Shag is in good hands. Ellen and Mrs. Garrity are
taking care of him." Charlie smiled and Pedro nodded
his head slowly, as though relieved of a great worry.

"I'll be in debt when I get out. I'll have to earn some
money," he said.

"You can work at the Bar L," Charlie said. "I
have to shove off now, but I'll be back to see you." He
got to his feet and smiled down at Pedro. "Get that
chin up and keep it up." He turned abruptly and left
the cell.

Charlie was buried in dark thoughts as he walked
down the street to the stable. There was one other
place where he could look for clues. He should have
thought of it when he was on Willow Creek. He should
have stopped at the cabin where Dillon was killed.
Colby had gone over it carefully, but he might have
missed something. Perhaps Seller was living out there.
Charlie had not seen him in town. It was too late to
ride out that night. It would be close to midnight
before he could get there. He decided to ride to the
ranch and leave from there. He could get a half night's
sleep that way.

There was plenty of time to think on the long ride to the ranch. But thinking did not get him any place. He was convinced that Dowd and Lester were mixed up in the killing with Seller. He was sure they had killed Dillon for the horse money and had framed Pedro. But as long as they stuck together, there was no hope for Pedro. He arrived at the ranch at one o'clock in the morning. He had eaten nothing since morning and headed straight for the kitchen as soon as he entered the house. He found a cold roast in the refrigerator and made himself a sandwich. He was munching hungrily and drinking milk when the kitchen door opened and Ellen stood blinking at him, muffled to her chin in a woolly robe.

"I heard you come in," she said in a low voice.

Charlie lowered the three-decker sandwich he was eating.

"I tried to be quiet," he said and smiled.

"I wasn't asleep." Ellen moved to the table and sat down.

"Want a glass of milk?" Charlie got to his feet.

"Yes," she said. "Then I want to talk."

Charlie set a glass of milk before her. He sat down and picked up his sandwich, taking a big bite. Ellen watched him.

"You've had nothing to eat all day?"

"I wasn't really hungry until I got into the house," Charlie explained. Ellen propped her elbows on the table and sighed deeply.

"I got to the horse range too late," she said slowly. "They had already fought."

Charlie stopped chewing and waited for her to go

on with the story. He knew from her face that it was
going to be bad.

"Golden Boy drove Prince off, but he is badly hurt.
It's his shoulder." Her eyes became misty. "He can
hardly walk."

Charlie set the sandwich on the table and pushed
it away from him. He was no longer hungry. A broken
shoulder could mean the end of the golden stallion,
and he had let it happen. He had gone off looking for
clues and had accomplished nothing.

"Was Prince hurt?" he asked.

"No," Ellen said.

"Then he'll be back to finish it."

"Shag and I stampeded him downcountry, but he
may not have gone far. Shag fought him." Ellen's eyes
lighted as she remembered the scene on the rim of the
canyon. "I was planning to leave here in about an
hour." Her voice trailed off.

"I'll catch a couple of hours sleep and then ride up
there," Charlie said.

"I'll go with you. I'll leave a note for Ann." Ellen
jumped to her feet eagerly. "We'll be in time to stop
another fight."

Charlie did not tell her that Prince would likely
work at night rather than by day. If he were coming
back, he would not wait for daylight. He smiled at
her.

"Glad to have you go along."

Ellen hesitated. "And Shag is gone," she said mis-
erably. "I saw him running across the cow pasture
toward the foothills just before dark. I think he's looking for Pedro."

Charlie grunted as though he had been hit hard in the mid-section. Trouble seemed to be piling up. Tex would be furious if Shag was running in the high country. Then the thoughts of both were clear to each other. They were thinking of the boy in Colby's jail.

"You didn't find any evidence?" Ellen asked.

Charlie shook his head. "It's like butting your head against a stone wall. I'm certain Seller is our man, and there must be a way to trip him up."

"If he stole Dillon's money, he may start to spend it," Ellen said hopefully.

"He's probably too smart for that." Charlie quickly told her about his trip to the cabin and to Cedar Bank, and of his meeting with Dowd and Lester. "They're both typical saddle tramps," he added. "But they don't seem to have a criminal record. Colby has a bulletin out on them and he's waiting for returns."

After Ellen left, Charlie sat staring at the inch of milk left in his glass and at the half-eaten sandwich. He dreaded what he would find when he reached the high range in the morning. There was no way to cast or splint a broken shoulder bone. The rule of the West was a mercy bullet fired into the brain. Charlie had seen Shorty do it. He had once done it himself. He got to his feet, his lips tight.

"If it has to be done, I'll do it myself," he said in a whisper.

8. To the Victor

ANN CARTER awakened from a light sleep and smelled coffee. When Ann returned to the ranch the previous night, Ellen had told her everything that had happened on her trip to the horse range. Ann lay for a few minutes thinking, then got up without wakening her husband and slipped into a dressing gown. Downstairs, she found Ellen in the kitchen cooking hot cakes. A pot of coffee was perking on the back lid of the range.

"Charlie got back," Ellen explained before Ann could say anything. "We're going up to get Golden Boy."

"Did Charlie learn anything helpful?" Ann asked.

"Nothing," Ellen answered. "But he's sure Dowd and Lester are mixed up with Seller." Ellen's eyes flashed. "That makes Seller the real killer, with those men helping him."

Ann sank down on a chair at the table. She had slept only fitfully and was weary. "I need a cup of coffee," she said.

"I'm sorry I wakened you." Ellen was contrite.

"You didn't waken me. I've been waking up every few minutes. This last time I smelled coffee and it seemed to be just what I needed."

Charlie came in as Ellen was filling his mother's cup. He was surprised and a little worried. "You shouldn't be up at this hour," he chided his mother.

"I can play night owl the same as you children." Ann lifted her cup and took a sip of the hot coffee.

Though he was worried, Charlie hungrily attacked the stack of cakes Ellen placed before him. Ellen ate slowly and she took only two cakes. It made Charlie feel guilty, but he knew he'd have a hard day and would need the cakes.

Ann did not object to Ellen's going with Charlie. When she was Ellen's age, she was riding night herd and making long trips alone, with only the stars and her horse's good sense to guide her. Ellen would be safe with Charlie. She liked the idea of their facing problems together. And she refrained from asking about Golden Boy. She knew very well what the verdict could be.

Charlie and Ellen left the ranch at exactly three that morning. Charlie set a fast pace until they reached Roaring River Canyon, where the trail was shrouded in black gloom. The roar of the river filled the dark void, and the horses picked their way carefully up the narrow rocky trail. Trey Spot sure-footedly led the way, with Diamond close behind her.

The bright starlight which flooded the bench above the canyon brought welcome relief to horses and riders. Already there was a faint flush in the eastern sky, hinting at dawn. The grass was laden with dew that glistened like hoarfrost, and the air was chilly. It was a time of day that Charlie liked. As they moved up toward the breaks, the cry of an old wolf rang down from the palisades above them. It was a lean, hungry cry and there was a lot in it that disturbed Charlie. Charlie knew that the old she-wolf was not hungry. This was the time of plenty for the killers. The cry was repeated and Charlie caught himself listening for an answer. If there was a male within hearing, he would answer that call.

"Wolves?" Ellen asked as she moved Diamond closer to Trey Spot's shoulder.

At that moment a chorus of yelps and howls rang out. Charlie glanced upcountry briefly.

"An old she and her dog wolves. I'd say there were four pups almost as big as she is," Charlie answered.

"They always send a chill down my spine," Ellen said with a shudder.

Charlie did not answer. He was listening to another voice coming from below. It was deep and throaty, and it was answered by the she-wolf. Then there was a bedlam of wild yelping which moved away down the mountain. It sounded very much like an old lobo routing the pups so that he could court the mother. Charlie did not try to deceive himself— the lobo's call was not quite true wolf.

Dawn was breaking when they reached the mesa where the mares usually fed. The pale light failed to reveal any horses. Charlie looked hard, but all he saw was a shimmering expanse of dew-heavy grass.

"They aren't here," Ellen said in dismay.

"Golden Boy probably moved them," Charlie answered quickly.

They crossed the park and halted close to the dark avenues of spruce. They would have to wait before they could pick up the trail of the mares. Impatience surged through Charlie. He wanted the light to come quickly, yet he dreaded what it might reveal.

The sky turned slowly to silver and then to crimson. The reflected light revealed two does feeding at the upper end of the park. Each had a fawn at her side. The does kept lifting their heads and slanting their long ears, listening and looking for the approach of a cougar or a wolf.

Charlie touched Trey Spot's flanks with his spurs and she moved toward the timber. When she was close to the black masses of shadow under the trees, he turned her aside and skirted the woods. He finally located the trail of the mares. It headed up out of the park. All signs indicated that the mares had gone unwillingly. They had bunched and many of the tracks indicated speed and dodging, as though the mares had been trying to escape punishment. Charlie was now thoroughly alarmed. He urged Trey Spot forward at a fast pace, keeping a sharp watch for signs of a fight between Golden Boy and the white stallion. What he feared was that he would find the big palomino down, a battered victim of an attack.

They passed through a dense stand of spruce

and came to another meadow. Here they came upon four mares feeding close to the timber. There was no sign of Golden Boy or the other mares, but their trail led east. Charlie took up the trail, with Ellen riding close beside him. They soon came upon six more of the herd. It seemed to Charlie that Golden Boy had probably started the mares moving and had lost control of them. They had scattered when they discovered that he could not control them. Locating them would take time and a lot of riding.

Pushing on, they came to a stream. They were now trailing no more than five horses. Rounding a cliff shoulder, they saw Golden Boy. He was standing chest-deep in a pool behind a rock ledge. He lifted his head when he saw them. Without thinking, Charlie whistled. Golden Boy nickered eagerly in response. Charlie sent Trey Spot charging toward the pool. Shaking loose his rope, he swung it and dropped a loop over the stallion's head.

"Come on out, big boy," he called gently.

Golden Boy hobbled out of the pool and stood waiting while Charlie dismounted. Ellen was already on the ground. She ran up to the big stallion.

"Careful!" Charlie warned.

Ellen stopped and waited until Charlie was beside her. He removed his gloves and began probing the swollen shoulder with his fingers, searching for ragged bone ends. The swelling was too deep for his fingers to discover anything. He patted Golden Boy on the neck.

"You're going to the ranch with us," he said.

Golden Boy snorted and shook his head. He was frustrated because he had been unable to keep his herd together, but he still had plenty of spirit.

"Is it bad?" Ellen asked.

"I don't know," Charlie admitted. "There's too much swelling to allow much of a check."

"Perhaps it's just a bruise," Ellen said hopefully.

Charlie mounted Trey Spot and headed her down the stream at a walk. Golden Boy hobbled along behind the mare, with Diamond and Ellen bringing up the rear. Charlie watched the big horse closely. The leg appeared to be useless. Golden Boy walked along on three legs.

The going was very slow, with many stops to let the stallion rest. Charlie knew that it would be an all-day job getting home. Rounding up the mares would have to wait. He wondered if he dared leave them an extra day while he rode over the mountain to Seller's cabin.

They rode slowly across a bench above Roaring River Canyon, skirting a heavy stand of spruce. Suddenly a gray form burst from a thicket and raced toward them. It was Shag, and he yelped eagerly as he bounded to meet them. He seemed overjoyed at finding them.

"Where have you been, Shag?" Ellen called.

Shag jumped up against her stirrup and barked. Looking at the dog, Charlie decided he had been running a long time without food or rest. His sides were gaunt, and there was a tired sag to his head. Wolves run down by dogs always had that sag, as though they were too weary to hold their heads up.

"You had better stay at home from now on," Charlie warned.

Shag moved out ahead, but he did not run. He trotted just in front of the horses, and kept looking back over his shoulder.

The passage through the canyon was very slow and very painful for Golden Boy. He was no longer the sure-footed wild stallion he had been. Evening was settling over the home meadows when they left the narrow gorge. Shorty Spears and Tex Malone were at the saddle house when they rode in. They both came to the corral gate and looked Golden Boy over. Shorty made a careful examination but offered no opinion.

"Put him in the small corral. I'll blister that shoulder with white liniment," he said.

Tex shrugged his shoulders. He frowned as his eyes followed Golden Boy through the corral gate. "This means we have to shoot or trap that white stallion before he drives the mares over the mountain and out of the country," he said grimly.

"We'll trap him," Shorty said eagerly.

"Will Prince round up the mares?" Ellen asked.

Shorty grinned. "He wouldn't be worth catching if he didn't round them up."

"He may decide to stay," Charlie suggested hopefully.

"Not likely," Tex answered. "I don't know where he came from, but I'd guess it was far south, possibly across the border."

Ellen went to the house with Shag at her heels. Charlie stayed with Shorty. He wanted to be with the great horse that had shared so many of his adventures. Shorty worked white liniment into the swollen shoulder. Golden Boy did not flinch. He seemed to know that his friends were doing what they could for him. When Shorty finished, he wiped his hands on a rag and stepped back. He shook his head slowly.

"Only time will tell. But one thing is sure: every wild range stallion comes to the same end. Meets a younger hoss and goes down fighting."

"He's not down and he isn't out," Charlie said harshly, but he turned away quickly. Golden Boy's head was up and he was looking toward the mountains.

For a few minutes Charlie felt hot anger against the white stallion. It faded as he rubbed Trey Spot down and cared for Diamond. They would trap the big stallion and tame him. And they had to save Pedro. Getting him free was more important than saving a herd of horses. He decided to visit the Dillon cabin the next day. He had faith in Colby as a sheriff, but this was something the sheriff had never had to deal with. If it had been horse or cattle rustling or a gun fight between two cow hands, Colby would know exactly what to do. But he was pitted against three cunning crooks who had planned their crime ahead of time.

As Charlie neared the back door, Shag came bounding down the steps. Mrs. Garrity had fed him, and all his weariness had vanished. He danced around Charlie eagerly.

"You better stay away from that she-wolf," Charlie

said gruffly. He rumpled Shag's fur and pulled one
ear. He decided that he would take more interest in
the dog from now on. He'd try to fill in for Pedro. He
would take Shag with him when he went to check the
Dillon cabin.

Grandby was seated in the living room with Ann
and Ellen when Charlie entered. He paused inside
the dining-room door, aware that they were talking
about him. The sudden silence when he appeared had
tipped him off. He smiled and tossed his hat on a
chair.

"Go ahead, don't mind me," he said stiffly.

Ann smiled gently up at Charlie. "We have been
wondering if you can accomplish anything by playing
detective," she said and patted the space beside her.
"Sit down, son."

Charlie glanced at his father and at Ellen. He
realized that there had been a difference of opinion
among them. There was a flush on Ellen's cheeks and
a glint of determination in her eyes.

"There does not seem to be anything you can
prove," Grandby said.

"There might be something," Ellen insisted as she
turned quickly toward Charlie.

"The important thing is that I have to try." Charlie
spoke slowly, trying to make them feel as he did.

"That's what I mean," Ellen said.

"We're in a tight spot here on the ranch," Grandby
reminded him. "We have a herd of valuable mares
scattered over a rough range where a wild stallion
runs. It is almost a certainty that he invaded our range

to find mares, and that when he has rounded up a herd, he'll head back to wherever he came from. If he drives them across the border into Mexico, we may never recover them." Grandby's mouth had taken on the stubborn twist Charlie knew so well.

"I know all those things," Charlie said. He glanced at his mother. She was looking out the window and seemed lost in thoughts far from their problems.

"We have riding to do," Grandby went on. "The beef steers need attention, and we have to shove the cows up to the high-grass range. Those things have to be done on a ranch."

"I want one more day. Tomorrow." Charlie faced his father and their eyes met.

Grandby frowned. He liked to treat Charlie as his partner, but he still thought of him as just a boy who should do as his father wished. Grandby was a careful man who liked to have things run smoothly, and he never took chances. He always settled matters in what he considered was a reasonable way. He bowed to forces he could not master, instead of fighting back blindly.

Charlie's father frowned and shook his head. "You want to play detective tomorrow. You expect Tex and Shorty to finish the trap you started building. The cattle will be neglected, and you will have accomplished nothing."

Charlie flushed. He met his father's eyes squarely. "Do you agree with Pedro's lawyer that he should plead guilty?" he asked.

This sudden shift in the discussion jarred Grandby

and made him feel uncomfortable. He did not want to discuss Pedro. He cleared his throat.

"I agree with Mr. Hansen," he said stiffly.

"I told Pedro to refuse to plead guilty," Charlie said defiantly. "Why make a marked man out of him? He's not guilty."

"Now, now." Anger was edging Grandby's voice. "Pedro is only a sixteen-year-old boy. If he pleads guilty, I may be able to get him paroled in my custody. If he is convicted, he'll get a harsh sentence and have to serve his time."

"He'd be a self-confessed killer," Charlie retorted bitterly.

Ann saw that her husband and her son were headed for a serious break. She wanted to compromise, but before she could speak, Grandby said harshly:

"If I refuse to allow you to waste any more time looking for clues, what do you propose to do?"

Charlie hesitated only a moment. "I'm riding over to the Dillon cabin tomorrow. I'm going to keep on trying until I've tried everything."

Color mounted in Grandby's cheeks. Ann spoke sharply. Ellen had moved away from the two men and seated herself across the room. Ann's eyes were flashing and both father and son knew she was really angry —something that rarely happened.

"You can just stop fighting each other," she said. "I agree with Charlie—Pedro cannot plead guilty. He's innocent and that is the strongest defense anyone can have. This is one time we do not compromise." She looked straight into Grandby's eyes, and his flush deepened. "We can handle the problems here on the ranch. And the least we can do is to stick together on this." She paused, her chin up.

Charlie wanted to rush across the room and hug his mother; instead, he remained where he was and watched Grandby. Grandby's lips moved and finally he started to smile. He had met Ann at a rancher's picnic. She had blown up and waded into two cow hands who were abusing a stubborn horse. Seeing her angry had won him. He considered her the most beautiful woman in the world when she was angry. Seeing the smile on his father's lips, Charlie relaxed.

Ellen did not know what to do. She seemed to have become a stranger in a circle where she had always been a member. She watched the faces of the family fearfully. Once she started to get up and run to her room, but her knees turned weak and refused to support her. Finally she managed to find her voice.

"I guess I'll go to my room," she said.

Grandby was suddenly all concern. He laughed and crossed the room to slip an arm around Ann. Then he faced Ellen.

"No need to run away, Ellen, the blow is over," he said. "As usual my wife is right. There will be no more arguments. Charlie will go look for clues. The boys will look after the mares and finish the trap. I'll handle the beef."

"I'll help the boys," Ellen offered eagerly.

Supper was forgotten. Mrs. Garrity had been listening inside the dining room and did not protest. Ellen moved close to Charlie and spoke in a low voice.

"Your mother is wonderful," she said softly.

Charlie smiled. "She's really the boss around here when the chips are down," he said with feeling.

They were silent for a long time. Ellen sat on the davenport and Charlie joined her. Tex and Shorty came in for supper and Mrs. Garrity poked her head through the doorway.

"Better come eat," she said.

9. Blind Alley

BEFORE SADDLING Trey Spot the next morning, Charlie went to the corral where Golden Boy was kept. He stood outside the corral for a few minutes looking at the big fellow. Golden Boy was propped on three legs at a feed rack. So far as Charlie could see, the swelling had not gone down, and the stallion seemed to have lost a lot of his fire. Charlie dreaded what the next few minutes would reveal. As soon as he moved the big horse, he would know if there was a broken bone. It had been impossible to tell before, but now that the leg had stiffened, he would be able to detect a break. Charlie thought of calling Shorty but decided against it. If the death sentence was to be imposed upon Golden Boy, he would do it himself.

Charlie turned away from the corral gate. He knew he was stalling. Down at the barn, Tex and Shorty were busy getting the trail wagon loaded and ready

110

for the trip into the high country. Ellen was with them, but not helping much. Charlie turned abruptly and reached for the gate. He swung it open and entered the corral. Golden Boy turned his head and looked at Charlie, but he did not move. Charlie walked up to him and halted. He raised one hand and brought it down sharply across Golden Boy's rump. With a startled snort the big horse turned around. Charlie's eyes were on the swollen shoulder and on the leg. The leg moved stiffly, but it moved. It did not drag limply. Golden Boy seemed surprised because the leg worked. It was the first time he had put any weight on it. Charlie laughed, a shaky relieved laugh. The shoulder bone was not broken. Golden Boy might have to favor that leg always, but he would be able to use it.

Charlie's first eager relief faded as he considered what it would mean if the stallion did have a game leg. He wouldn't be able to take care of a band of range mares. He'd be a corral stallion and that would be tough on a horse that had always known the freedom of the hills. Charlie left the corral and saddled Trey Spot.

Ellen came over to stand beside Charlie as he tied his slicker and lunch back of the saddle. He had strapped on his gun belt and was carrying a Colt. He did not know exactly why he wanted to pack a gun. He never carried one except when he was riding a dangerous horse like Ace.

"I'll take Shag with me," Charlie said. Shag was standing close to Ellen. He knew that a trip was in prospect, and he was eager to be off.

"He lived over there when Pedro was working with Dillon," Ellen remarked thoughtfully. "He might help you."

Charlie had not thought of that angle. He grinned at Ellen. "I'll keep an eye on him when we get there."

Shag was reluctant to go with Charlie. He wanted to stay with Ellen, but when Charlie rode away and whistled for him, he followed. Ellen made it clear to him that he was to go with Charlie.

"Good luck!" she called after them.

"I'll need it!" Charlie called back.

When he reached the top of the ridge above the ranch, Charlie looked back and waved his hat. Ellen returned the wave with her scarf. Trey Spot moved over the rim and they were alone, with Shag running ahead. As Trey Spot climbed up the steep trail to the divide, Charlie went over all the facts he knew about the Dillon killing. Pedro had arrived at the cabin about five o'clock in the evening and found Dillon dead on the floor with Pedro's gun beside him. Pedro had picked up the gun and handled it. He had knelt beside the body to see if Dillon was alive. While he was kneeling with his back to the door, Seller had arrived and jumped him. Shag had come to his rescue and they had escaped. Charlie was sure that was the true story of what had happened.

The coroner had placed the time of death as after four o'clock, but he was not a medical doctor; he was one of Cedar Bank's dentists. There was a possibility that he was wrong. Dillon might have been killed earlier, but even if he had died around four o'clock, Seller could have done it and stayed out of sight wait-

ing for Pedro. Dowd and Lester gave him a tight alibi
as to time. Sheriff Colby reported that the cabin had
been searched thoroughly. Floor boards had been
pulled up and mattresses cut open. Pedro said he had
not noticed the condition of the cabin.

Charlie admitted that circumstances were all
against Pedro. He had quarreled with Dillon. The
murdered man had given him a raw deal by cheating
him out of his share of the horse money and even selling Pedro's own saddle horse. And Pedro had had the
opportunity. The jury might refuse to believe that
his gun had been stolen. It was Pedro's word against
the three men—Seller, Dowd, and Lester.

Charlie had a feeling the cabin might hold some
clues. There might be some evidence that the sheriff
had missed. He might find something that would
indicate that Seller had gotten Dillon's money. Better,
there might be some small thing that would help break
Seller's alibi. If that alibi wasn't cracked, Pedro would
be convicted.

When they reached Willow Creek, Shag began to
show excitement. The dog knew that they were
headed for the cabin, and hoped to find his master
there. Charlie called him back and Shag stayed close
to Trey Spot, but he whined impatiently and kept
sniffing the air and looking ahead. After an hour of
staying close he suddenly broke into a run and vanished into a willow thicket. Charlie called to him, but
Shag did not come back. Charlie gave Trey Spot her
head, and she galloped after the dog.

They broke through a stand of willows and Charlie
saw the cabin. It was a low log building with a dirt

roof. He set his spurs and forced a burst of speed from Trey Spot. Seller was standing in the doorway of the cabin, and he had a six-gun. Shag was leaping about, snarling at the man. Seller was trying to draw a bead on the dog.

"Shag! Here, boy! Down, Shag!" Charlie shouted as he slid his own gun from its holster.

Shag whirled and looked toward Charlie. Seller also looked.

"Put up that gun!" Charlie shouted.

Seller hesitated, his eyes on Charlie's Colt. Trey Spot came to a sliding halt. Seller lowered his gun. Shag moved close to the horse and stood watching the man in the doorway. A deep growl rumbled in his throat. Charlie swung down from his saddle and shoved the Colt into its holster. Seller watched, an angry scowl on his face.

"What you want here?" he demanded.

"I was riding this way and thought I'd stop." Charlie realized that was a lame explanation. He had not expected to find Seller at the cabin. He had been sure that the state witness would be in town. "I thought you'd be in Cedar Bank for the hearing," he added.

"Ain't needed yet," Seller said. He was watching Shag warily. "You keep that dog away from me or I'll shoot him."

"He thinks Pedro is in the cabin," Charlie said. He took a step toward the doorway, but Seller did not move.

"You're not wanted around here," Seller said.

Shag had stretched out on the ground. His neck

scruff was still lifted, and he kept his eyes on Seller. Charlie was certain that Seller was the killer. If Shag hated him, he was bad. Charlie shrugged his shoulders and turned toward Trey Spot.

"Thanks for the hospitality," he said grimly.

Seller laughed harshly. "You and your old man are trying hard to get that greaser kid off the spot. He killed my partner, and I aim to see that he's put away. But you won't get to plant any phony evidence around here." Seller balanced his .45 menacingly. "Get going."

Charlie mounted Trey Spot. There was no point in arguing with Seller. Shag got to his feet and followed Charlie as he rode away. They traveled down the creek until the willows hid them from Seller's view. Charlie looked the lay of the land over carefully. There was a thicket of cherry and wild plum back of the cabin. If he used it for cover, he might be able to reach the cabin's one window without being seen. He decided to try. Dismounting, he hitched Trey Spot in a stand of hemlocks, then placed a hand on Shag's head.

"Down, Shag," he ordered and pressed on the dog's shaggy head.

Shag sank onto a bed of needles and looked up at Charlie. His tail thumped the ground, but he made no sound, and he did not move when Charlie started to leave.

"Stay here," Charlie ordered. He wasn't sure that the dog would understand or obey, but he had to try. It would be risky to approach the cabin with

Shag at his heels. Shag started to rise. "Down, Shag!" Charlie ordered sharply. Shag sank back and placed his muzzle on his forepaws.

Charlie walked out of the grove. He stopped to look back. Shag had not moved. He understood what Charlie wanted him to do. Charlie circled through the timber above the cabin. He was about to leave cover and start across the meadow where the cabin stood when Seller appeared. He had a saddlebag in his hand, and he walked quickly across the meadow below the cabin. Charlie saw a horse picketed close to a clump of willows. Seller stopped beside a big pine and picked up a saddle and blanket. He took a bridle from a limb and headed toward the horse. Charlie turned and trotted back to Trey Spot. Seller was getting out, and he would see Trey Spot if he rode down the creek.

Shag was still lying waiting as Charlie entered the grove where Trey Spot stood. Hastily Charlie unhitched the mare and mounted. He sent her into the timber at a gallop. Shag followed, keeping close to her heels. When he was several hundred yards above the creek, Charlie halted and watched the trail below. Seller rode into view at a gallop, heading down the creek.

Charlie felt let down. He was sure that Seller was taking important evidence away with him. There probably would be nothing left in the cabin for him to find. Seller might have Dillon's money in his saddlebag. Charlie considered riding after him and forcing him to open the bag. That would mean holding Seller up at gun point. He decided against it. But he would have a look inside the cabin. He waited ten minutes, and then rode down to the cabin. Dismounting, he stepped through the open door.

Shag followed him inside and went straight to one of the bunks, where he sniffed and whined. The cabin was bare. There did not seem to be any place to hide anything. There was nothing in the cabin aside from the furniture, except three cans of beans on a shelf above the stove, and a few cooking utensils. Charlie lifted a blanket on one of the bunks and saw that the straw mattress had been slit open. The rip had been fastened together with a couple of rusty nails. Some of the floor boards looked as though they had been pried loose and pounded back into place again.

Charlie stayed a half hour in the cabin looking for a place where a man would cache his money. He found nothing. Shag had stretched out beside one of the bunks and seemed prepared to wait there.

"Time to go, boy," Charlie said.

Shag's tail thumped the boards, his big brown eyes looked up at Charlie, but he did not move.

"Come along, we're leaving," Charlie said coaxingly.

Shag remained where he was. He lowered his head to his forepaws and whined. Charlie stepped over to Shag and bent down. He caught the dog by the scruff of his neck and pulled him to his feet. Shag whined, but he did not resist. Charlie led him outside and closed the door. When he released his grip, Shag followed him across the yard to where Trey Spot stood waiting.

Charlie mounted Trey Spot and whistled to Shag

as he sent the mare away from the cabin at a lope. Shag hesitated for a few moments, then followed. Charlie glanced back at the dog. His tail drooped dejectedly and he kept looking toward the cabin.

When they were two miles above the cabin, Shag moved out ahead of Trey Spot and ran freely. Charlie decided that the next time he visited Pedro he would take the dog along.

Their pace slowed as they started the steep climb up to the divide. It was an hour past noon, but Charlie had not thought about his lunch. He remembered it when Shag flushed a snowshoe rabbit and furiously pursued the big-footed bunny. The rabbit eluded Shag by crossing him up in a dense thicket. Charlie halted beside a small stream and whistled to Shag. He dismounted and untied the lunch pack from in back of the saddle. Shag loped in from the woods and lay down at his feet. Seating himself on a grassy hummock, Charlie opened the lunch. He took a thick beef sandwich from the package. He removed the lettuce leaf and laid the sandwich before Shag.

"Better than raw rabbit," he said.

Shag sat up quickly. He sniffed the sandwich and deftly removed the meat, which he swallowed at one gulp. He ate the bread more slowly. Charlie grinned as he punched holes in a can of orange juice with his knife.

"You'll get a stomach-ache gobbling your food that way," he said.

Shag's tail thumped the ground, and he eyed the lunch package eagerly. Charlie took a deep drink of juice, then got out another sandwich. He did not bother to remove the lettuce when he handed it to Shag. Mrs. Garrity had packed four sandwiches and a waxed-paper bag stuffed with meat scraps. Charlie wanted only one sandwich, so he gave the last one to Shag. He kept the bag of scraps for the dog's dessert. He felt he had missed a lot by never having a dog. He could blame Tex for that. Tex had convinced him that a dog was a dangerous nuisance on a ranch. He decided that when Shag left, he'd get a dog. Then the thought struck him that Shag might stay on the Bar L a long time. There would be no place for him to go if Pedro was sent away.

Charlie reached the ranch before five o'clock. He cared for Trey Spot and went to the house. He knew his mother had seen him arrive. She spent a lot of time at the big front window. She would want to know what he had found.

She was in the living room. He sat down and told her all that had happened. When he finished, she was more excited than he had expected.

"You learned a lot," she said. "Seller probably had the money right there in the cabin and took it away in the saddlebag. He certainly acted like a guilty man."

"I'm sure he's guilty, but I handled it badly. I should have spied on him before letting him know I was around," Charlie said glumly.

"We have to find a way to prove the things we are sure of," Ann said. "There has to be a way. A man can't get away with murder."

"I suppose I should have trailed him and found out what he did with that bag," Charlie said.

"He's bound to make a misstep. You must tell the sheriff about your visit to the cabin."

Charlie walked to the wall phone and called the sheriff's office. Colby jumped to the conclusion that Charlie was trying to get in touch with Grandby Carter and said that he had stopped by early that morning to see Pedro. Charlie interrupted to state the reason for his call and then told about Seller's leaving the cabin with the saddlebag. Sheriff Colby did not try to hide his irritation at Charlie's playing detective.

"Why don't you leave such matters as checking on Seller to me?" he said gruffly. "Any man starting out for town would take his saddlebag if he was going to stay over a day or so, or if he was leaving the cabin for good."

Under any other circumstances, Charlie would have accepted the sheriff's statement without question. He admitted to himself that it was a flimsy clue, but somehow he felt sure that the saddlebag held the key to the mystery of Dillon's murder. As a law-enforcing officer, Charlie realized, Colby was interested in concrete evidence—not in the hunches of a teen-age boy. He could see that it was useless to argue further with Colby about Seller and the saddlebag.

"I'll keep an eye on Seller if he shows up in Cedar Bank," the sheriff finally promised.

Charlie had to be satisfied with that. Glumly he hung up and turned to his mother.

"I don't think I accomplished much," he said. "And I've been neglecting my work at the barn. Guess I better catch up on some of the work there."

He got to his feet and reached for his hat. What

he really wanted was to be down at the barn when Ellen and the boys arrived.

Charlie visited Golden Boy first. The big stallion moved in a jerky walk when Charlie slipped a halter on him and led him around the corral. The swelling had receded somewhat, but it still was impossible to tell whether there was a pulled tendon or just a bad bruise. Charlie left the corral and busied himself around the barn and saddle house. Shag stayed close to him and seemed to be interested in everything that Charlie did. The supper hour arrived and the party had not returned. When Mrs. Garrity called him to supper, he went reluctantly. While he was washing up in the room next to the kitchen, she looked in on him.

"Your father hasn't gotten back from town. Ellen and the boys will be late. Shorty said they would work until late and make a night ride home."

Charlie smiled. Trust Mrs. Garrity to get the plans out of Shorty. There wasn't much that went on she didn't know about.

After supper Charlie sat on the front porch waiting for the party. He heard them coming long before they reached the corral. He and Shag hurried down to meet them.

Ellen was the first to ride in, followed by Shorty. Tex arrived five minutes later. Charlie got in the first question as Ellen dismounted.

"Is Prince still up there?"

Ellen laughed. "He's up there and he's about finished rounding up the mares."

"And he's acting mighty restless," Shorty added.

"What did you learn?" Ellen asked.

"Not much. I'll tell you the whole story after you've eaten." Charlie leaned against Diamond and jerked the cinch free. He stripped off saddle and bridle and took them to the saddle house.

"You didn't find any clues?" Ellen was matching Charlie's stride as he turned back to rub Diamond down.

"I guess not, but I am sure now that Seller is our man," Charlie replied. "You better run along to the house. I'll be up right away."

Ellen went reluctantly, and Shag went with her, romping around her playfully. He was very happy to be with her. Shag liked and respected Charlie, but he loved Ellen.

When Tex arrived, he cared for his horse and went straight to the bunkhouse without a word. Shorty waited and talked with Charlie.

"We may have trouble getting that horse into the trap," he said. "He may decide to leave these parts before we drive."

"Is that what's eating Tex?"

"I reckon so."

"Could we herd the mares and hold him with them?" Charlie asked.

"Not that boy. He holds them close to timber or the rim of a canyon. Our only chance is to catch him when he has them close to the canyon where we built the trap." Shorty shook his head. "He's a lot of horse, smart as a fox."

"That could take time," Charlie said thoughtfully. "And it's risky."

They had reached the house, and Shorty headed around toward the back door. He planned to slip into the washroom without being detected by Mrs. Garrity. It was a daily game they played, and one in which Shorty was usually the loser. This time he again was unsuccessful. Mrs. Garrity intercepted him in the hall. As Charlie entered the front room, he heard Mrs. Garrity firing questions at Shorty. He couldn't hear Shorty's answers, but knew he was replying. Charlie wandered around the front room, then finally went out on the porch to wait for Ellen. While he was waiting, his father drove up and parked the Buick at the front gate. When he reached the steps, he sat down beside Charlie. Charlie told his father what had happened at the cabin.

"Nothing that can be used," Grandby said. "We need more than circumstantial evidence."

"What did you learn?" Charlie asked.

"Colby keeps his opinions to himself. Hansen is still skeptical of Pedro's story, but he's the best lawyer we can get. Cedar Bank lawyers do not get a chance to learn much about criminal defense. I saw Seller with Dowd and Lester while I was eating in the café. They seemed to be celebrating." Grandby frowned grimly.

"Spending a lot of money?" Charlie asked eagerly.

"No, but I'd say they were planning a big party for tonight," Grandby said. "I couldn't give Pedro much encouragement. He's too smart to swallow anything but the truth."

"I'm taking Shag with me the next time I go to town," Charlie said.

"Good idea." Grandby got to his feet and walked into the house. Charlie sat looking at the stars until he heard Ellen's footsteps. He was glad she was coming. He felt very low at the moment. She sat down and looked up into his face.

"Now tell me everything," she said eagerly.

Charlie told her his story. When he finished, she was silent for a time. Finally she said:

"Seller is guilty. And he won't get away with it."

Charlie was thoroughly tired of hearing people say that Seller couldn't get away with it because he was guilty. Guilty men sometimes did get away with crimes.

"He'll get away with it if we don't get a break," Charlie muttered gloomily.

"No, he won't," Ellen said firmly. "And don't you go getting discouraged. You learned a lot today."

Charlie stared off into the night and they both were silent for a long time. There wasn't any need for talk. It was good to have Ellen there beside him. He began to feel a little better.

10. Clues

THE TRAP was finished and its gate stood open; a section of the lower barrier was ready to be installed at a moment's notice. If the white stallion drove the mares down the canyon when no one was there to spring the trap, the horses would pass through it without realizing it. Charlie and Ellen kept watch on the herd, waiting for the hour when Prince would have his charges in position above the trap.

The white stallion was as wary as a cougar and as smart as a fox. Charlie and Ellen watched him through field glasses for hours. They did not risk moving in close enough so that he would be aware of their presence. They wanted him to feel that he was secure. If he felt safe enough, he might relax his vigilance. He was having a very bad effect upon the mares. Under his savage leadership they were becoming more and more like wild horses every day.

He was a rough dictator who brooked no breaking of his rules. When he screamed an alarm, the mares were instantly on the alert. Twice Charlie and Ellen watched him stampede the herd into a canyon in a mad charge that threatened legs and necks. Each time there appeared to be no cause for alarm. Prince just seemed to be indulging a wild whim, or else he was putting the herd through a drill.

Twice daily Charlie spent a half hour with Golden Boy. The shoulder swelling had gone, but the leg was still stiff. Charlie exercised the stallion in the hope that the leg would limber up and become useful. Shorty always shook his head and offered no encouragement. Time alone would tell whether Golden Boy was to be a cripple. The big horse fretted and chafed and worked his way slowly up and down the corral trying to get loose so that he could return to the high country.

Shag went everywhere with Ellen, but Charlie knew he was running at night. If Tex was aware of it, he said nothing. He ignored the dog, and this suited Shag, because he had never made friends with Tex.

Pedro had been held for trial after Grandby had demanded a hearing rather than a commitment to juvenile custody. Pedro had stood up in court and said that he was not guilty as charged. Judge McHenry had set a trial date. At the hearing the district attorney had called only two witnesses—Seller and Sheriff Colby. But Dowd and Lester were in court, so Pedro's attorney did not make a point of Seller's alibi.

From the beginning the sheriff had worked on the theory that Pedro had the Dillon money. He had tried every way he knew to get Pedro to give him a hint as to where the money was hidden. The district attorney was backing this idea. He was convinced that Pedro was guilty and would come after the money when he had finished serving his term.

At first Colby would not let Charlie bring Shag to the jail. It was part of his plan for breaking Pedro down to a point where he would confess. He also limited visitors. He finally admitted that either the boy was a good actor or else he did not know where the money was. Pedro could have shot Dillon and afterward failed to find the money. The sheriff pointed out that Seller's arrival had probably cut the search short. Charlie's arguments did not greatly impress Colby. He knew that Grandby had originally agreed that the boy should plead guilty.

Charlie talked to all the cow hands he knew who had met Seller and his alibi men. He was hoping that one of the men might have said something that would discredit their story. It was Shorty's idea that men like Seller, Dowd, and Lester are always boastful when drinking. But no one had heard them brag and when they talked about the murder, they always told the same story.

Finally Colby told Charlie that he could bring the dog in the next time he came. The sheriff had suddenly lifted all restrictions on visitors, and had stopped asking Pedro where he had hidden the money. The day of the trial was drawing near, with conviction almost a certainty.

Ellen rode into town with Charlie the day he took Shag to visit Pedro. Charlie took the precaution of putting a collar and a leash on Shag before he let him out of the car. He wasn't sure the dog had ever been in a town before. Shag might panic and run for the mountains.

Ellen handled the leash when they let Shag out of the car on Main Street. Shag showed more surprise at the collar and leash than he did over the cars and the people he met along the street. Everyone looked at him suspiciously, and most of the people they met shied away from what appeared to be a big gray wolf, even though the wolf was being handled easily by a slim girl who weighed no more than a hundred pounds.

The instant Shag entered the jail he caught Pedro's scent and sprang toward the hallway leading to the cell, dragging Ellen after him. He almost knocked Colby over as he bounded past the sheriff. He leaped up against the bars of the cell and licked Pedro's hands and face. When Colby opened the cell door, Shag leaped into Pedro's arms. They both sank to the floor and Pedro buried his face in Shag's furry neck. His shoulders shook as he clung to the dog. Ellen looked at Charlie, and he knew she was going to cry. She brushed past him and walked down the hall and out of the jail. Finally Pedro looked up at Charlie. His eyes were moist, but he tried to smile.

"He has been treated well," he said gratefully.

Pedro was pale and thin; his eyes looked much too big for his face. He nodded toward his cot.

"Use the cot. Shag and I will sit on the floor."

His shoulders shook as he clung to the dog

Charlie sat down. It angered him to see how the boy was wasting away. His excitement at seeing Shag was the first interest he had taken in life since Charlie had begun visiting him in the cell. Pedro was stroking Shag's head. He looked up at Charlie.

"You have found nothing new?"

"Nothing," Charlie answered frankly. "But I haven't given up trying."

Ellen returned to the cell. Her face was composed, and there was no trace of tears. She smiled down at Pedro and Shag.

"You make a fine-looking pair," she said.

"Want us to ask the sheriff if we can leave him with you?" Charlie asked.

"No," Pedro said quickly. "He must learn to live on the ranch, and he must forget me."

"Bunk!" Charlie exploded.

"He cannot go to reform school with me," Pedro pointed out.

"You're not going," Ellen said fiercely.

Pedro gave her a wan smile. "You are good friends," he said sadly. "But I am going. I will be there until I am twenty-one."

"You're not going," Charlie said. "We'll get you paroled to my father."

"I could not come to you," Pedro said. "Not as a parolee."

"Seller is the criminal; even Shag knows that," Charlie argued.

"Seller always hated Shag." Pedro smiled faintly. "Shag liked Dillon even if he was dishonest, and Dil-

lon liked Shag. Seller was afraid of Dillon. He would
have shot Shag if he hadn't feared Dillon."

This was the first time Charlie had had a chance to
question Pedro about Dillon's saddlebag. He knew
the sheriff did not attach any importance to it, but he
was still interested.

"What sort of container did Dillon keep the money
in?" Charlie asked.

"He kept his money and papers in a brown leather
case in his saddlebag," Pedro answered.

Charlie jumped off the cot. "I saw Seller leave the
cabin with a leather saddlebag," he cried.

"We have to find it!" Ellen urged.

"Seller had a leather saddlebag," Pedro said. "It
was smaller than Dillon's bag, much smaller." He
shook his head. "Seller would destroy Dillon's bag.
What you saw was his own."

"This was a large bag and it had what looked like
a large brass clasp on it." Charlie looked at Pedro ex-
pectantly.

For a moment hope flickered in the boy's eyes. "Dillon's bag had a large brass clasp," he said.

"I better get on this," Charlie said. He turned to
Ellen. "You visit with Pedro until I get back."

Charlie hurried out of the jail and headed for the
livery stable. He found the same boy in charge who
had taken care of Trey Spot when he first visited
Pedro. The boy sat on a packing crate in front of the
stable.

"I'm Charlie Carter," Charlie said.

"Of the Bar L." The boy smiled. "I've seen you ride

in the big race at the cattlemen's show. Won a dollar on you." He flicked an oat hull from his sleeve. "I'm Buck Elder."

"Do you know a man named Seller?" Charlie asked.

"Sure I know him. He owes the stable four dollars."

"He came in from the south end of the county a while back, remember?"

Buck nodded. "That's when he stuck us."

"He had a brown saddlebag with him. Know what he did with it?"

"Packed it off with him. Said he had his razor and stuff in it." Buck grinned. "But I don't think he ever shaves."

"The boys usually leave their saddlebags with you, don't they?" Charlie asked.

"Sure." Buck jerked his head toward the office door. "We got a big old safe in there. Used to be in Matt's store. If they got valuables, we lock 'em in that safe."

"Know where Seller stays?"

"Probably on Third. Lots of cheap rooms over there," Buck answered.

Charlie thanked Buck and left. He headed for Third Street, a shabby avenue of old houses. He remembered seeing ROOMS FOR RENT signs on many of those houses.

At the third shabby house, the landlady said that Seller was staying there.

"He owe you money?" she asked sharply.

Charlie shook his head and smiled. "Does he owe you money?"

"He's back on his rent," the woman replied sourly.

"Those saddle tramps have a way of taking off in the night." Charlie's smile widened. "But he has baggage you can hold."

The woman laughed harshly. "He has two saddlebags, both of them empty." She shook her head sadly. "Both together not worth a week's rent."

"I'd like to see them," Charlie said.

"You want to buy them?" the woman asked eagerly. It was clear she did not think her chances of getting any money out of Seller were very good.

"They may be worth his back rent," Charlie said.

"If they are, you get them and he goes out tonight." The woman turned toward the door. "Come along and look at them."

She led Charlie to a small ground-floor room and opened the door without knocking. Charlie was close behind her when she entered the room. This could be the break they needed. The woman opened a closet door and bent forward. Her voice was angry as she turned around. She was holding a small battered saddlebag.

"The big one that looked pretty good is gone. I'll bet that bum pawned it for liquor money." She held the bag toward Charlie. "This one worth anything to you?"

Charlie shook his head. He had missed again. Seller had disposed of the bag which could have been identified as belonging to Dillon. He had a feeling Seller hadn't pawned it. There was only one place in town where money could be gotten on pawned goods, and that was the proprietor of the poolroom.

"When did you first look inside the bags?" Charlie asked.

The woman tossed the empty bag into the closet. "Couple of days ago," she said. "But I'd moved them when I cleaned the room. Moved them quite a few times. The big bag was heavy. I was sure I'd find something in it."

Charlie turned toward the door. The woman hurried after him.

"What do you want with him? If you're going to give him a job, I want you to help me get my money."

"I'm not giving him a job, but he will have some money coming in a few days. He's a witness at a trial. You go talk to Judge McHenry." Charlie smiled at the woman.

Charlie walked out of the rooming house and returned to the jail. Colby was working on some papers in his office. He heard Ellen's laugh coming from the cell down the hallway. Charlie stepped into the office. He sat down at the sheriff's desk. Colby glanced up at him.

"The boy has perked up some," he said.

Charlie nodded, then he started telling the sheriff about the missing saddlebag. The sheriff listened without interrupting him. When Charlie finished, he leaned back and reached for his pipe.

"You've sort of picked Seller." He located his tobacco pouch and filled his pipe. He did not say anything more until he had it lighted. "He's a saddle tramp. Says he's broke. His story is that he lost his share of the horse money playing poker with Dowd and Lester. That could be so. Those boys seem to have money to spend. All three are tramps, but they all tell the same story and are willing to get up on the stand and swear to it under oath. It will be up to the jury to decide whether they're lying, or for the judge to decide if the jury is waived by the boy's lawyer."

"What do you think?" Charlie asked.

"I was sure the kid shot him," Colby said. "Now I don't know."

"Seller wants everyone to think he's broke," Charlie said stubbornly.

"I'll keep the saddlebag in mind, but I have only one deputy and he's up north on a case. I can't do any storybook detecting." Colby spoke mildly and without much enthusiasm.

Charlie got to his feet. He felt completely frustrated. He was so convinced that Seller was the murderer that he couldn't understand why the sheriff doubted it. He walked back to the cell. Pedro was seated on the bunk beside Ellen. Shag lay at his feet.

"Time to go?" Pedro asked.

"I'm afraid so," Charlie said.

The brightness left Pedro's face. He stood up and bowed to Ellen. "It was so good of you to come. I know you'll look after Shag."

"I'll keep him safe for you," Ellen promised. She picked up Shag's leash and pulled gently. The dog got to his feet. He looked up at Pedro and wagged his tail.

"Go with Ellen," Pedro ordered. "And mind what she tells you."

Shag walked ahead of Ellen out of the cell. It was as though he understood every word Pedro said.

Charlie followed Ellen. Pedro did not walk through the open door of the cell. He stood watching them as they left the jail.

"Shag and I would like hamburgers," Ellen said when they were on the street.

Shag started tugging at his leash. He sniffed buildings and hitch-rack posts and fire hydrants. He had never encountered evidence of so many other dogs in his life. The news excited him greatly.

Charlie took them to a hamburger stand. He ordered two hamburgers with all the trimmings and two plain ones. The fry cook looked down at Shag.

"Where'd you catch the lobo?" he asked.

"We're keeping him for a friend," Ellen explained.

The fry cook made Shag's hamburgers extra large. After he had watched the dog devour the first one in two bites, he fixed a third.

"This one's on the house," he explained to Charlie and Ellen.

With the hamburgers and pop finished, they walked to the car. When Charlie opened the back door, Shag jumped in. Charlie removed the collar and tossed it on the back seat. Shag yawned hugely. The three hamburgers had made him drowsy.

Charlie headed the car out onto the mountain road. Ellen was silent for a long time. Finally she spoke and her voice was touched with anger.

"The judge could have let him out on bond. It's criminal to keep a boy in a cell like an animal."

"Judge McHenry is a stickler for the law," Charlie explained. "This is a murder charge. If Pedro was older, he would be facing the electric chair."

"It's terrible." Ellen's voice was trembling.

"The worst part of it is that I've fallen on my face every time I've had a chance to help," Charlie said bitterly. "I fumbled everything at the Dillon cabin, then I didn't have sense enough to follow up. Seller took that saddlebag to his room and he had it there quite a while. I'll bet he even had the money and Dillon's papers in it."

"You're not a detective," Ellen said gently. "The next time you won't miss. But I didn't know about his having the bag at his room."

Charlie told her about his experience with the landlady at Seller's rooming house and his talk with the sheriff. The ride home wasn't a very happy one.

11. Night Raid

CHARLIE DECIDED that the time had come to saddle Golden Boy and test his ability to handle himself. The swelling had left the injured shoulder, but the leg was stiff. If that stiffness could be worked out of the muscles, Golden Boy would be fully recovered. There was only one way to get the leg loosened up, and that was to ride the stallion. Golden Boy was beginning to show signs of temper at being held in the small corral. He seemed to sense that the white stallion had taken over leadership of the band of mares. The instant Charlie hit the saddle Golden Boy started to buck. But he did not have the catlike speed to put on much of a show. As they passed Shorty, he called to Charlie:

"Let him have his head. It may loosen up his shoulder."

When the reins loosened, Golden Boy lowered his head and tried to toss Charlie out of the saddle. When he failed to unseat his rider, the big horse settled down and ran. Charlie kept him out a half hour, but when he returned, he wasn't sure the shoulder muscles had loosened enough to enable the stallion to take care of himself on the range. Charlie would have to wait and see how Golden Boy acted after a number of workouts.

Ellen was at the gate when they rode in. "He looks good," she said.

"He's mean as a bear with a sore head," Charlie answered. "But he's not up to taking on Prince yet."

"Shorty says Prince drove the mares through the trap last night," Ellen said eagerly.

"Good stuff." Charlie grinned down at Ellen. "We may take him any day now."

Ellen's face clouded. "Not until after the trial, I guess."

"Wish Pedro could be here to help." Charlie leaned down and opened the gate. Golden Boy reared and lashed out at the bars with his forefeet. He laid back his ears and screamed loudly.

"Good boy," Charlie shouted. He let the stallion feel the spur rowels and Golden Boy moved into the enclosure. Charlie called back to Ellen. "Will you close the gate?"

Ellen closed the gate and Charlie unsaddled the stallion. When he slipped the bridle off, Golden Boy limped to the fence, where he stood snorting and looking up toward the mountains. Charlie swung the saddle over his shoulder and headed for the saddle house. Shag appeared from a shady spot beside the building. He yawned and wagged his tail. Charlie frowned at the dog. Shag had certainly spent the night running in the hills. He had a gaunt, tired look about him.

"I have to ride the upper drift fence today," Charlie said. "It hasn't been checked in weeks. It will be plain, hard work." He smiled at Ellen.

"I'm helping Ann make a new dress," Ellen said.

Charlie got the saddle that he always used on Trey Spot and went out to catch the mare. He saddled her and rode away from the ranch. He was a mile from home before he thought about Shag. The dog had not followed him as he usually did when Ellen wasn't riding. He probably had decided he'd rather sleep after running all night.

The day was uneventful. Charlie mended several breaks in the drift fence and checked the high-country beef steers. The ride was a long one, and he made the last five miles by moonlight. He was nearing the home pastures when he heard the old she-wolf and her pack. She was roaming well below her usual haunts in the breaks. Charlie shifted his course and rode past the slopes where the calves were held. All was well there. Groups of cows with white-faced calves at their sides fed peacefully or lay chewing their cuds. Charlie sat listening to the hunting call of the wolves. The old she-wolf had shifted direction and was heading back up the mountain. Charlie decided the calves were in no danger. He headed Trey Spot toward home.

Down at the ranch, Shag heard the hunting cry of the wolves, and it stirred him to action. He loped out across the home meadow toward the hills, passing under the wire fence a half hour before Charlie reached the gate.

Shag ran by sound, swinging along with powerful strides. He headed for the calf pasture because the calls were coming from a ridge above it. Instinct told him that he had a job to do. The she-wolf was well out of bounds. This was cattle range, and the wolves had no business being there.

By the time Shag reached the pasture, the she-wolf and her pack were already there. The old wolf had scented the calves and knew that an easy kill awaited her. She burst out of the timber, with her dog wolves fanned out behind her. Their red tongues lolled over white fangs and their amber eyes gleamed in the moonlight. The cry of the kill rose in a chorus of savage yelps.

The cows took alarm, but there was little they could do to protect their calves. They had been shorn of their only defenses—their horns—and their clumsy hoofs were worthless as weapons. The calves scattered or bunched in groups of shoving, wiggling bodies. The she-wolf headed for a group of five calves huddling against a bank. With her pack at her heels she descended upon the helpless youngsters. Her long fangs hamstrung a calf and slashed its throat as it went down bawling and kicking. The young wolves swarmed over the other calves, slashing and ripping. The taste of warm blood filled them with a frenzy to kill. Two of the calves managed to scramble up the bank and escape slaughter.

Shag arrived as the carnage was at its height. Forgotten was his brief romance with the big wolf. Unerringly he launched his attack upon her. His heavy body hit her and rolled her over. As he lunged for her

throat, she leaped to her feet and dodged. She lashed
out and her fangs ripped his shoulder. She was startled because another wolf was attacking her instead
of joining her in the kill. Once before she had ignored
the man smell on this big lobo; now she recognized it
as a deadly sign.

The young wolves stopped worrying the calves and
stared at the stranger whom they had always hated.
Shag whirled from the mother and charged them.
They scattered, but Shag slashed one of them across
the tendons of a hind leg. The young wolf howled and
staggered away, dragging one leg. The young wolves
broke for the timber. Shag let them go. He was after
the old wolf.

He caught up with her in a clearing, well inside the
woods. When she saw that she could not outrun him,
she made her stand. A warning snarl passed her
parted lips. She knew she had to kill this man-loving
wolf or die herself. She was not a coward, but she
would have retreated if there had been an avenue of
escape. When Shag lunged at her dog-fashion, seeking to close with her, she leaped aside and lashed out.
Shag whirled and charged again. This time she
ducked the other way, and again she lashed out, grazing Shag's throat with her fangs. The third time she
ducked, Shag was ready for her. He made a fast shift,
changing position with her, and he was upon her, his
fangs reaching for her throat. She fought savagely, but
he was inside her guard, and his teeth had sunk
through the fur of her throat and into her flesh. They
closed like a vise, and all her desperate lunging and
struggling could not loosen them. Slowly her strug-

gles lessened, and her body went limp. Shag tossed her from him and stood over her, snarling savagely. He was at that moment a killer filled with blood lust.

The young wolves had halted in the woods to watch and wait. They were filled with a strange fear, and they did not know what to do, because the old wolf did not come to lead them. Shag saw them and leaped toward them. They scattered and raced up toward the sanctuary offered by the barren breaks. Shag followed one of them for a short distance before turning back. He returned to the body of the old wolf and waited there for a long time. Always before, when he had made a wolf kill, Pedro had come and praised him. When no one came, he left the dead wolf and loped homeward. Two hours later, after licking his shoulder wound, he was sound asleep on a pile of sacks inside the door of the saddle house.

The next day Charlie and Ellen rode to the high range to check on the white stallion and the mares. They found the herd at a spot close to the trap. Charlie was tempted to put up the lower barrier and let Ellen wait at the gate to spring it shut while he stampeded the herd. He finally decided against it. It would be wiser to wait until the entire Bar L could help with the drive. Prince would not be easily driven.

"It's tempting," he told Ellen, "but we better wait until we have a crew."

They were watching Prince through their field glasses. He stood on a low ridge above the meadow where the mares were feeding. A stiff wind swirled his mane and tail into a white cloud. His head was up, and his ears propped forward. One of the mares, a two-year-old, had moved close to the woods. She seemed nervous and kept jerking up her head as she worked her way toward the timber. Suddenly the white stallion was after her. He thundered across the meadow, and cut her off before she could reach the stand of aspens she was headed for. His teeth closed upon her neck and she almost went down. Whirling, she shook herself free. His teeth found her rump and sank deep. An instant later his big body hit her and she went to her knees. The stallion's hoofs beat at her as she staggered to her feet. His angry scream rang across the meadow. The little mare galloped toward the herd crowding together in the center of the meadow. They lifted their heads nervously and shifted about, but the stallion did not bother them. He turned and trotted back to the ridge.

"He's cruel!" Ellen said between clenched teeth.

"He's too rough for ranch mares," Charlie admitted. "That filly will be marked for life. Dad won't like it at all." He was thinking that it would be a pleasure to teach Prince a few of the rules of ranch life.

"We ought to trap him right away!" Ellen exclaimed angrily.

"Not many of the mares will try to get away from him," Charlie said.

The day was spoiled for Ellen, and they started home early. When they reached the ranch, they found Tex and Grandby down at the barn. Charlie was surprised to see Shag chained to a hitch ring on the saddle-house wall. The dog wagged his tail and looked up at Ellen hopefully. Charlie and Ellen hurriedly dismounted.

"What's wrong?" Charlie nodded toward Shag. "Why the chain?"

Tex furnished the answer. "There's three dead calves up in the calf pasture, ripped by wolves." Tex jerked his head toward Shag. "His tracks are all over the place along with the wolf tracks. No mistaking them with that lame foot."

"It looks bad," Grandby said. "I rode up there and looked the ground over."

Charlie wet his lips. He needed time to think. He didn't know what to say, but he refused to believe that Shag was a calf killer, no matter how many tracks there were in the calf pasture. Ellen knelt and put her arms around Shag's neck. She looked up at Tex defiantly.

"He didn't kill any calves." Her voice was tight with anger.

"I'll have a look myself." Charlie spoke gruffly as he turned to Trey Spot.

"Go ahead," Tex said grimly. "Take a good look."

Charlie turned back from his horse and faced his father and the range boss. "You'll do nothing about the dog until I've checked. If he's to be shot, I'll do it." It was not a request; it was a flat order that even Tex understood. Tex shrugged his shoulders, Grandby frowned.

"No one said anything about shooting him," Charlie's father said. "But it would be better than keeping him chained. A wolf dog chained goes bad in a hurry."

"He won't be chained," Ellen said. She stood up

and faced the men. "I promised Pedro I'd take care of him, and I will."

Grandby wasn't prepared for Ellen's flat statement. Tex said nothing. He felt he was right and that Grandby would have to go along with him. Grandby tried to smooth things over.

"It may be just temporary," he said.

Ellen gave Shag a pat on the head, then walked past the men and up the path to the house.

Charlie mounted Trey Spot and rode away. As he galloped along, he was thinking that about everything that could happen in the way of bad luck had happened. He was certain that Tex and his father had seen Shag's tracks at the scene of the kill; he knew that the dog had been running at night, and he was sure that the dog had met the she-wolf. But he wanted to see for himself.

When he reached the scene of the kill, he dismounted and examined the carcasses of the three calves and the ground around them. It was difficult to determine the amount of the kill the wolves had eaten. They had been followed by coyotes, so that there was little left except hide and bones. He found Shag's tracks in soft earth close to the carcasses. Coyote and wolf tracks were mixed up around the dead calves. The higher ground nearby was harder and showed no tracks. Charlie knelt and studied the signs, looking for evidence of a fight. He found none. There was no wolf hair on the bushes and no spot where the grass had been trampled. He shook his head and frowned. He knew the evidence he was looking at would convince Tex and his father, but it did not completely satisfy him.

Mounting Trey Spot, Charlie circled around the spot where the kill had been made. He found no tracks because the ground was dry and hard and he saw no signs of a struggle. After riding around for almost an hour, he headed Trey Spot toward home.

As he left the scene of the kill, he saw two coyotes peering over a hill. They were eager to worry the bones and clean them of any remaining scraps of

meat. That was the way of the coyote and the buzzard, undertakers of the air and the thicket.

Supper that night was a quiet affair. Grandby had told his wife about the calf kill and she was upset. She had developed a strong liking for Shag. Charlie had told Ellen what he had seen, and what Tex and his father believed. Ellen refused to believe that Shag was a calf killer.

Mrs. Garrity came into the dining room with a bowl of noodles. She set the bowl down with a thump and surveyed the faces around the table.

"I may as well take a vacation from cooking." She looked squarely at Grandby Carter. "Anyone with good sense knows that dog isn't a stock killer. You just put that into your pipe and smoke it." Having relieved her mind, she stamped off into the kitchen.

Grandby laughed and the tension eased a little. Charlie finished his supper and went out to sit on the porch steps. Ellen did not come out to join him. She went up to her room and stayed there.

Charlie saw Mrs. Garrity come out of the back door. She had a bowl in her hands, and she marched down toward the barn. Shag wouldn't go hungry, no matter what happened to him, as long as Mrs. Garrity was their cook.

Dusk settled and the moon rose. Charlie got to his feet and walked down to the saddle shed. Shag sat mournfully looking at the bowl of meat and noodles Mrs. Garrity had set before him. Ordinarily the bowl would have been licked clean. Tonight Shag wasn't hungry. He had barely touched his supper. Charlie knelt beside the dog and slipped an arm around him.

"Tough break," he said.

Shag's tail thumped the ground and he tried to lick Charlie's cheek.

Charlie was thinking of Pedro. If the decision was to destroy the dog, it would be hard to tell Pedro. He had a feeling that this would be a harder blow than being sent away to reform school. He stayed a half hour with Shag, then visited Golden Boy.

The stallion was restless. He pawed the ground with his sound leg, and nickered. Charlie patted his neck and talked to him. Golden Boy refused to be consoled. He wanted to get out of the corral, and head for the high country.

"You better work the kinks out of that leg," Charlie said grimly.

As though in answer, Golden Boy moved across the corral. He put his head down and lashed out with his heels, then whirled and charged back across the corral.

There was no light on in Ellen's room. Charlie went to his room and undressed. An hour later he was still wide-awake and staring at the ceiling. The empty bed across the room kept reminding him of Pedro, and when he thought of the boy, he thought of his dog.

12. Justice

ONE DAY of being chained to a wall showed what would happen to Shag if he was denied the freedom to run. He lay watching everyone who passed. He allowed Charlie to pat his head but failed to respond. With Ellen he was eager and excited. It was clear that he expected her to free him. She put on his collar and leash and took him for a long walk. Tex and Shorty stayed away from him. They were convinced that he would turn mean and dangerous.

Grandby took his time arriving at a conclusion regarding the dog. When he decided, he told Charlie.

"If Judge McHenry sends Pedro to the reform school, we will destroy the dog. I'll wait until the trial is over. If Pedro is freed, he can take the dog with him when he leaves."

Charlie had been expecting such a decision. He knew that it was reasonable, but he resented it.

"Pedro will stay with us if he is cleared," Charlie said.

Grandby shook his head. "Not if his dog has to be chained and cannot run with him when he rides."

"I think he'll stay."

"There are other reasons," Grandby said. "Pedro asked me to do several things for him if he is sent away. If he is freed, he will do them himself."

Charlie knew his father would say no more. He would not betray a confidence Pedro had placed in him. Charlie felt a little hurt because Pedro had confided in his father but had told him nothing. They were standing at the corral gate. Charlie turned and looked at Shag. The way things looked now the dog was doomed. His father's voice broke in on his thoughts.

"Judge McHenry has delayed the trial as long as he will. He did it because I asked for delay. The dog will have to remain on a chain until after the trial."

Ellen was walking down the path toward the barn. Charlie waited for her. She halted and smiled at Shag. He got to his feet eagerly. Ellen had a cloth and a small bottle of iodine in her hand. Charlie stepped closer as she knelt beside Shag. The dog looked up at him and a growl rumbled in his chest.

"Behave yourself," Ellen said gently. "As soon as I fix your cut, we'll go for a walk."

Charlie watched her swab the cut with iodine. Shag did not flinch when the iodine entered the wound. His tail wagged and his jaws sagged open.

"There," Ellen said as she finished. She looked up

at Charlie. "What are you going to do with him?" she asked.

"If Pedro is freed, he can take Shag away with him."

"And if he is sent away?" Ellen's blue eyes searched Charlie's face.

"Dad will get rid of Shag." The instant the words were out of his mouth, Charlie was sorry he had been so blunt.

Ellen got to her feet. "You don't believe Shag killed those calves?"

"No," Charlie admitted, "but that isn't enough to convince my father and Tex."

"We have to find a way to convince them." Ellen rested a hand on Shag's head. "There must be some way."

"There is only one way," Charlie said. "I'll have to find evidence that Shag fought those wolves."

"What will you look for?"

"A dead wolf would do the trick," Charlie said grimly. "The catch is that I haven't been able to find a dead wolf. I've searched pretty thoroughly near the spot of the kill."

"Shag might have chased the wolf a long way before catching it," Ellen said thoughtfully.

Charlie nodded. "Might have run it several miles."

"You'll find that dead wolf."

"There's one other chance, a slim one," Charlie said thoughtfully. "If I could sight that wolf pack and the old she-wolf wasn't with them, I'd be able to put up a good argument."

"We have to get them to give Shag another chance. He should not be chained to a post." Ellen spoke with determination.

"I'm riding up to the horse range. Want to come with me?" Charlie asked hopefully.

"I better take Shag for a long walk. I can't stand seeing him lying there with that chain keeping him from moving about."

Charlie nodded. Ellen was right, Shag needed exercise and attention to keep him from turning mean and savage. Charlie turned away and walked toward the corral where Golden Boy stood looking over the fence. The stallion came eagerly to the corral gate, expecting to be freed from his prison. He was full of life, but he still favored the injured leg. Charlie watched him for a while. A few more days might see the limp vanish. There was no way of knowing. He left the corral and saddled Trey Spot.

Once Charlie was in the saddle and galloping away from the ranch buildings, some of the tension that had gripped him dissolved. The jolting action was like a tonic to his tight nerves. When he reached the foothills, he let the mare set her own pace.

By the time he reached the mesa above Roaring River Canyon, he knew that he could not ride away from the problems facing him. They rode with him, and he could not forget them even for an hour.

Charlie rode on into the rough breaks until he spotted the ranch mares. He sat on a ridge screened by young pines, and studied the herd through his glasses. The white stallion was very much in charge. The mares were all restless, probably wanting to go to water, but held back by the stallion. Charlie noted that they were feeding less than half a mile above the trap. Things were working out as planned. This was a perfect spot for a wild stallion to hold his herd. The tall-grass meadows were close to an avenue of escape—the canyon which led down into wild country.

Suddenly the white stallion decided to humor the mares. With a loud call he galloped toward them. Instantly they closed ranks, and headed toward the rim of the canyon. Prince paced down upon them, his ears back and his teeth bared. The mares broke and charged over the rim into the canyon. For an instant the white stallion stood poised on the edge of the steep slope, his head up, his mane and tail flowing in the wind; then he plunged after them. Charlie took a deep breath. He had just watched a beautiful bit of drama. But it would have been more satisfying if Golden Boy had been driving the mares.

Charlie did not ride directly back to the ranch. He circled across the beef range. The sun was hot and the air was filled with the spice of spruce and pine sap freed by the heat. An eagle soared on motionless wings in the sky above, and a cock grouse drummed in a thicket. Charlie rode down a long park following a murmuring little stream. Everything was right in the world, except for him and those close to him.

The sun had set by the time Charlie halted Trey Spot at the home corral. Shag lay beside the wall of the saddle house. He did not turn his head to welcome Charlie, and his tail did not move. Charlie dismounted and cared for his horse. The family and the boys were at the supper table when he entered the kitchen. He washed up and joined them. Ann smiled at him, but it was Ellen he looked at. Ellen gave him a questioning smile.

"How are the mares?" his father asked.

"Fine," Charlie answered. "Prince is using the canyon as a trail to water."

"Good," his father said.

"Did you see the wolf pack?" Ellen asked.

"No sign of them."

Tex gave him a quick glance, then went on eating. After that, there was little talk. Shorty finished his supper and mumbled as he excused himself. Tex followed him a few minutes later. Ellen pushed aside her dessert.

"I'm sorry," she said to Ann. Charlie's mother was looking at Ellen's plate. The girl had eaten almost nothing. "I'll take a walk before dark." She arose quickly and went into the kitchen.

Ann Carter looked from her son to her husband. "I'll be glad when this strain is over," she said.

Grandby nodded. Charlie pushed back his chair and got to his feet. "We've let everybody down,"

Charlie said bitterly. Before either his mother or father could speak, he strode out of the room.

Charlie knew where he would find Ellen. She had gone to the kitchen to get food for Shag. He walked down the path to the corral and found Ellen sitting on the ground watching Shag eat his supper. He sat down beside her.

"I looked for those wolves," he said. "But I was late getting into the barrens and wolves hole up during the day."

"We'll get a break," Ellen said hopefully. "We just have to."

Charlie wished he had her faith. He knew he was going to keep on trying to save Pedro and Shag, but there was so little to give him any encouragement. They sat silently watching Shag finish his meal. After

he had licked the bowl clean, they walked back to the house.

In spite of his worries, Charlie slept well that night. His long ride had made him muscle-weary, but he was strong and healthy, and he awoke the next morning feeling fine. The good feeling lasted until he got to thinking about Pedro and Shag. He lay for a time trying to think of a way to trap Seller into betraying himself. He had just one day's time, but that would be enough if he had a plan. But he didn't have one, and he couldn't think of one. Charlie decided he would ride into Cedar Bank anyway and make one last attempt to trap Seller. Having reached a decision which promised some action, he got out of bed and dressed.

Shorty, Tex, and Grandby had already eaten breakfast and were off on various jobs. Grandby wanted to make a complete check of the cattle on the high range before going into town for the trial, which might take at least two days if Judge McHenry moved as cautiously as he usually did. Ann and Ellen were not up. Mrs. Garrity fixed Charlie's breakfast and he ate hurriedly. Before he left, he looked into the kitchen.

"I'm riding into town," he informed Mrs. Garrity.

She nodded grimly. None of the happenings on the ranch pleased her at the moment. She sloshed a dish into soapy water as Charlie closed the door.

"Anyway, he's trying to do something," she muttered to herself.

Charlie saddled Trey Spot and rode down the driveway. He could have driven the Buick, but he preferred the feel and the smell of a horse.

He kept up a steady pace and reached Main Street

by eleven o'clock. He rode past the jail without stopping. He didn't want to talk to Pedro. He was sure he couldn't get away with a lie. He pulled up before the poolroom and hitched Trey Spot there. He could make another try at getting something out of Dowd and Lester.

Entering the poolroom, he stopped at the cigar counter. There were only three men in the room, all strangers to him. The proprietor came forward.

"Hello, Charlie. What's on your mind?"

"Dowd and Lester been around?"

"Haven't seen them for a spell." The proprietor frowned. "Gave them notice to stay out of my place. They're card crooks."

Charlie left the poolroom. He knew he was just marking time, going through useless motions. He looked into stores and cafés as he walked down the street. He checked the bars and asked at a place or two, but he did not find the two men. Finally he walked over to Third Street and stopped at the house where Seller was staying. The landlady answered his knock.

"You," she said, then she added, "He's gone. Paid up and left."

"Do you know where he went?"

"He said he was going back to the hills to catch some wild horses." The woman's eyes searched Charlie's face. "But he'll be back for the trial of that murderer. He's a state witness."

Charlie thanked the woman and turned away. He decided he should stop at the jail. He found the door open. Colby was at his desk. He looked at Charlie without much interest.

"You haven't been around for a while," he said.

"Have Dowd and Lester left town?" Charlie asked.

"They're out on Sand Creek. Picked up a few days' work." The sheriff smiled.

"Seller is out in the hills," Charlie said.

"He'll be in tomorrow," Colby said. "He's set on seeing that boy sent up."

"Sure," Charlie agreed. "That would fix everything just right for him." He looked across at the sheriff. "You find any trace of that horse buyer?"

"Not a trace."

"What Dillon said to that horse buyer is the whole reason Seller framed Pedro. He was afraid Dillon had told the buyer a lot more than Pedro or he heard. Anyway, he said enough to point the finger at Seller, in case Dillon disappeared and anyone started asking about him or looking for him."

The sheriff frowned. "Several people have asked about Dillon. A brother in Santa Fe wants to know if there was any money recovered."

"Did any of them know Seller?"

"None of them ever heard of him." The sheriff grunted and shook his head. "You want to see the boy?"

"Yes." Charlie got to his feet and turned toward the hallway.

Colby got his keys and they went to the cell. Pedro was seated on his cot. He offered no greeting.

"Hello, Pedro," Charlie said as he entered the cell.

Pedro moved over and Charlie sat down beside him. He did not know what to say, but he had to say something.

"I'm still digging." The words sounded false and foolish.

"Thanks," Pedro answered.

Charlie hoped the boy would not ask about Shag. He hurriedly told Pedro about the white stallion and how he was using the canyon where the trap was built. Pedro listened but did not seem interested.

"He's a fine horse," Charlie said.

Pedro looked at the floor and said nothing.

"We'll catch him and gentle him," Charlie promised.

Pedro looked up. "I've caused you folks much trouble, but it will soon be over." Pedro's voice was low.

Charlie got to his feet. "Buck up," he said. "We're not licked yet."

"You have done more for me than you will ever know," Pedro said earnestly.

"See you tomorrow," Charlie said.

"Tomorrow." Pedro managed a smile.

Charlie wanted to get away. He'd done nothing for Pedro by visiting him. He had come empty-handed. He walked down the hall and out of the jail.

Charlie got back to the ranch before his father and the men returned. He found Ellen seated beside Shag in the shade of the saddle house. The dog seemed more like his old self. A plate beside him was licked clean. Ellen looked up at Charlie.

"Did you tell Pedro?" she asked.

"No." Charlie sat down beside her.

"I have figured out a way to save Shag," Ellen said softly.

"Good," Charlie said eagerly.

"I'll leave for home after the trial and take him with me. That is, if they send Pedro away."

Charlie stared at her. "But you were to stay all summer," he protested. Then he realized that by going she could save the dog. He shook his head. "It would save Shag, but you can't do it except as a last resort."

"I don't want to go," Ellen admitted. "But I'll do it if it is the only way to save him."

Charlie stared gloomily out across the meadow, a frown twisting his mouth. He could not argue with Ellen, but he was determined to make a final effort to keep both Shag and Ellen on the ranch. Ellen smiled at him.

"I think you'll find a way to clear Shag," she said. She got to her feet and Charlie stood up. They walked slowly up the path to the house.

13. Trial

WHEN ANN CARTER told her husband that if Pedro were sent away, Ellen planned to leave and take Shag with her, he protested:

"She has always been a good ranch girl. She should understand."

"I'm afraid that she doesn't understand," Ann said. "I guess at her age I'd have felt the same way."

"She is free to do as she likes," Grandby said stiffly.

At supper that evening Mrs. Garrity was the only cheerful member of the group. She was pleased with Ellen's decision. After supper Charlie went for a walk. He went over every possibility he could think of for helping Shag and Pedro but came up with no new ideas. He went up to his room and to bed without talking to Ellen.

The next morning Ellen and Charlie's mother got ready to go to town with Charlie and his father. Tex and Shorty were staying on the job. Charlie knew that Shorty would ride up to the horse range at least once.

The ride into Cedar Bank was a silent one. The hearing was set for ten o'clock and they were in time to get seats. Grandby sat at the counsel table with Pedro and the defense attorney, Mel Hansen. Most of the people in Cedar Bank had Pedro already convicted. For this reason, Grandby had consented to let Judge McHenry hear the case and decide without a jury. Sitting beside Grandby, Pedro looked little and forlorn. But he smiled at Ellen and Ann Carter. Mitch Seller sat at a table with the district attorney, George Kelly. He was wearing a fresh shirt and suit, and he was clean-shaven. He looked like a prosperous rancher. Charlie suspected that the prosecutor had made him clean up. The prosecutor was a thin young man who wore horn-rimmed glasses. He was not a very successful lawyer and was eager to make a showing as a county official. This was a juvenile case, but it was also a murder trial that had been talked about a lot.

Judge McHenry sat back of a large table. In a juvenile case the county judge had jurisdiction. Judge McHenry wasn't a lawyer, but he had served as county judge for twenty years, and in that time he had learned a lot of law. The judge called the court to order himself. Sheriff Colby sat behind Pedro and watched.

"This is a juvenile hearing and as such it will be informal," Judge McHenry announced. "It is the duty of this court to hear witnesses and to arrive at a just decision."

The prosecutor frowned. There was no doubt in his mind about the guilt of the defendant, or of his securing a conviction, but he wanted to get the most out of the trial. Judge McHenry regarded him silently for a long interval. Mr. Kelly thought he should speak up.

"May I remind Your Honor that this is a murder trial?"

"That will not be necessary, Mr. Kelly. The court is fully aware that a murder has been committed. However, we are dealing with a child."

"We are dealing with a murderer, Your Honor." Mr. Kelly's voice rose to a high pitch.

"Is that your opening statement, Mr. Kelly?" Judge McHenry asked mildly.

"It is not, Your Honor." Mr. Kelly turned slowly toward the table where Seller sat. He took his time sorting papers and finally selected several.

"I suggest that you state what you aim to prove." Judge McHenry leaned back and locked his fingers over his ample paunch.

Charlie looked around the room for Dowd and Lester. They were seated at the back of the room. He knew that they were there to back up Seller's story if it was questioned. They wouldn't be needed, of course, because Seller wasn't on trial. Mr. Kelly had turned to the judge. He cleared his throat.

"Your Honor"—Mr. Kelly glanced regretfully at the empty jury box—"I will prove that the defendant, Pedro Martinez, did on the twentieth day of June, 1956, cause the death of one Tom Dillon by shooting him in the head with the defendant's gun. I will establish that the two quarreled over money and that the defendant threatened to do what later he did in fact do, kill Tom Dillon. I will establish by eyewitness that the defendant was found kneeling beside the body of the deceased, holding a .45 Colt revolver. When the witness attempted to make a people's arrest, the defendant's savage dog attacked him. The defendant escaped and ran away. He did not voluntarily give himself up; he was apprehended by the sheriff." Mr. Kelly paused for breath, and the judge interrupted:

"There is no need for a formal, long-winded opening statement, Mr. Kelly."

Mr. Kelly colored and shuffled his papers. "Your Honor, it should be established that Tom Dillon had a considerable sum of money which disappeared and has not been found." Mr. Kelly turned and looked at Pedro. "I have no doubt the defendant took that money after shooting his victim."

"I suggest that you stick to what you can prove," Judge McHenry said dryly.

Mr. Kelly had no intention of leaving out any details which would add to his reputation as a prosecutor. "Your Honor, the matter of the missing money has a direct bearing. This boy"—Mr. Kelly turned and peered at Pedro through his thick glasses—"has admitted that he considered part of the money belonged to him, that he had been cheated."

Mr. Kelly turned to his table and picked up an ancient Colt revolver. He held it up so that everyone in the room could see it. Judge McHenry did not wait for Mr. Kelly's little speech. He said curtly:

"Mark the gun exhibit A."

The clerk of the court stepped over and took the

gun from Mr. Kelly. He released it reluctantly. Then he produced a bullet from an envelope and laid it beside the gun on the judge's desk.

"Mark the bullet exhibit B," the judge ordered.

Mr. Kelly was showing signs of frustration. He had planned a telling punch with each exhibit. He expected Mel Hansen to object to his references to the gun and the bullet, thus giving him an opening for an argument. Hansen didn't make a single objection, and the judge had ruined his performance.

"Are you ready to proceed with proof?" Judge McHenry asked.

"I have witnesses who will prove what I have said." Mr. Kelly knew he could not be stopped once he started questioning his witnesses.

"Proceed with them," the judge ordered.

The first witness was the coroner. He testified that death had been caused by a bullet which he had removed from the brain of the dead man. He wasn't sure of the time of death, placing it at about four o'clock in the afternoon. Hansen made no cross-examination.

The next witness was the sheriff. He had been told of the killing by Seller, and had ridden out with the coroner to the Dillon cabin. He identified the gun as the death weapon, having sent the bullet and the gun to the state ballistics laboratory. He described how the cabin had been searched by someone. He told how he had finally located Pedro, naming Seller as the man who had tipped him off that the boy was at the Bar L ranch.

Mel Hansen asked the sheriff a few questions. He

was interested in Seller and his movements on the afternoon of the killing. The sheriff told of checking Seller's alibi. He stated that he was satisfied with it.

Mr. Kelly next called his star witness, Mitch Seller. Seller took the stand with a flourish. He seated himself and stared at Pedro. After he was sworn, he identified himself as Tom Dillon's partner. Mr. Kelly told him to tell his story in his own words.

"Me and Dillon was running wild horses. We picked up this kid, and fed him, let him do chores for his feed and bed. He got the idea he ought to be cut in for a third. He had a big row with Dillon and threatened to shoot him." Seller glared at Pedro.

"Tell the court what happened on the afternoon of June twentieth," Mr. Kelly prompted.

"I was up at the KT camp, playing some cards with Ike Dowd and Pete Lester. I got home around five o'clock. The door was open, and when I looked into the cabin I saw Tom lying on the floor. The kid was kneeling beside him holding the .45 Colt he always packed." Seller hesitated.

"Then what did you do?" Mr. Kelly asked.

"I jumped the kid and took the gun away from him. I aimed to bring him to town. His wolf dog jumped me from behind and I had a tussle with him. The boy got away and the dog went with him."

"Then you rode to town and reported the killing to the sheriff?" Mr. Kelly asked.

"That's right. The kid stole a horse and made off." Seller let his eyes rove over the crowded room.

Mr. Kelly turned to Mel Hansen. "Your witness," he said with a flourish.

Hansen got to his feet. He stood looking at Seller for a few minutes. Seller stared back at him. Hansen stepped close to the witness.

"Where are those men who will swear that you were playing cards with them on the afternoon of the twentieth?" he asked.

"They are right here in court," Seller answered.

Judge McHenry interrupted. "Mr. Seller is not on trial, Mel."

"I am merely trying to assure myself that the witness is telling the truth. He had opportunity and he had motive—money. Unless it is clearly established that he could not have shot Dillon, then he is suspect."

"The sheriff satisfied himself," Judge McHenry pointed out. "If he had not been satisfied, he would have arrested the witness."

Mel Hansen knew that he was waging a losing fight. His only hope was that by placing Pedro on the witness stand he might be able to play upon the sympathy of the judge. He turned away from Seller. "That is all," he said.

"Do you have any witnesses?" Judge McHenry asked Hansen.

"I have one witness. Pedro Martinez."

"Pedro Martinez take the stand," the judge ordered.

Pedro got to his feet. He looked very small and much alone as he walked to the big chair beside the judge's table. When he sat down, his boots swung clear of the floor. The judge leaned forward and asked Pedro to raise his right hand. Pedro lifted a small hand, and the judge administered the oath. Hansen stepped close to the boy.

"Tell the court how you met Tom Dillon and Mitch Seller. Do not hold anything back. The court is interested in how they treated you, and all about yourself and them."

Pedro looked up at the lawyer. He started talking in a low voice, telling how he was hunting horses and how Dillon and Seller had moved in on him, offering him a third of the money if he would lead them to the wild horses he and Shag had located. He went on to tell how Dillon had sold his saddle horse along with the wild horses they had caught, and had not given Pedro any of the money. He told of the argument he had had with Dillon.

Hansen put in a question. "Did you threaten to shoot Dillon?"

"No, sir," Pedro said. "I told him that if I was big enough, I'd lick him."

There was a murmur of amusement from the crowd.

"Tell us about your gun," Hansen suggested.

"A week before Dillon was shot my gun disappeared. I seldom carried it with me. I usually left it at the cabin," Pedro answered.

"Did you suspect anyone in particular of stealing your gun?"

"It had to be either Mitch or Tom," Pedro said. "No one but them could have taken it."

"Tell the court what happened on the twentieth of June." Hansen stepped back from the witness chair.

Pedro was thoughtful for a moment. "I was out with my dog looking for wild horses. I got back to the cabin about five o'clock. When I went inside, I saw Dillon lying on the floor. My gun was beside him. I knelt down to see if he was alive. When I found he was dead, I picked up the gun and looked at it. Mitch Seller came in behind me and jumped on my back. My dog jumped him. I guess Shag would have hurt him bad if I hadn't called to him after I ran out of the cabin." Pedro stopped and glanced at Seller.

"Why did you run away?" Hansen asked.

"I knew I had been framed." Pedro looked straight at Seller and his chin was up. "I didn't think anyone would believe me." He shifted his gaze to his attorney. "I was wrong about that."

Hansen stepped close to Pedro again. "Did you kill Tom Dillon?"

"No, sir."

"Did you steal the horse money?"

"No, sir."

Hansen turned abruptly to Mr. Kelly. "Your witness," he said.

Mr. Kelly got to his feet quickly. He strode toward Pedro and halted before him. But he spoke in a friendly voice. He sensed a feeling of sympathy in the crowd which might also be shared by the judge.

"Do you want the court to believe that a small boy like yourself would be out alone hunting wild horses?"

"I have caught wild horses before," Pedro answered.

Mr. Kelly smiled. He seemed about to pat Pedro on the shoulder. "Indeed," he said. "And you acted as scout for Dillon and Seller?"

"Yes, sir."

"How old are you, Pedro?"

"Sixteen, going on seventeen."

"How much do you weigh?"

"Over a hundred pounds." Pedro flushed as he answered.

Mr. Kelly looked at the judge. "That will be all," he said.

Judge McHenry looked at the clock on the wall. The case had moved swiftly. It was one o'clock. He tapped the top of his desk with his fingers and seemed lost in thought. Charlie's heart tightened as he watched Pedro walk back to his place beside Grandby. He was sure that the judge had made his decision. The courtroom was still as the judge sat watching Pedro return to his chair. He leaned forward and spoke slowly.

"In view of the evidence I have no choice but to find you guilty, Pedro. I will see you in my office and tell you what I must do with you." He looked at Grandby. "Mr. Carter will come with you to my office and hear what I have to say to you." He glanced over the courtroom. "Court stands adjourned."

Charlie was watching Seller. The man was grinning broadly and shaking hands with Mr. Kelly. Anger surged up inside Charlie. He started to get to his feet, but felt a hand on his arm. Turning, he looked into the face of Sheriff Colby.

"Easy, son," Colby said.

"He's not going to get away with it." Charlie shook off the sheriff's hand.

Colby shook his head grimly as he turned away. The courtroom quickly emptied, leaving only a small group around the defense table. Seller joined Dowd and Lester at the door. They left the room together.

There were tears in Ellen's eyes. Ann Carter slipped an arm around Pedro.

"We're all for you, Pedro," she whispered softly.

Judge McHenry was gathering up the papers on his desk. The sheriff stood waiting. The judge stepped around his table. He spoke to Grandby. "Bring Pedro to my office." He glanced at the sheriff. "You can wait here, Sheriff." Grandby and Pedro followed the judge. Charlie left the courtroom with Ellen and his mother.

"He got a rotten deal!" Charlie burst out. "Seller got away with it!"

"Judge McHenry did what he believed was right," his mother said. "People believe Pedro did it. I could see it in their faces."

"How could they?" Ellen cried out. "How could they when they heard what Pedro said?"

"I should have socked that grinning crook," Charlie said bitterly.

"We'll wait for Grandby at the car," his mother said firmly. "When he comes, we'll have dinner."

It was an hour before Charlie's father joined them. He smiled when he saw the family waiting for him, but the smile faded at once.

"You should have gone to the café and eaten," he said.

"Do you think any of us would have an appetite until we knew what is to happen to Pedro?" his wife asked.

"I tried to persuade the judge to parole Pedro to me." Grandby slid in back of the wheel and reached for the ignition key. "He's afraid of public opinion, I guess. There's an election coming up. Pedro goes to the reform school with no recommendation for parole."

"There's one thing I haven't tried," Charlie said grimly. "That's beating the truth out of Seller."

Grandby looked at his son. "You better forget Seller." He smiled at his wife and Ellen. "No use making this a completely gloomy day. We'll go have dinner."

14. Secret of the Spruce

CHARLIE SAT on an overturned bucket outside the saddle house. His mood was one of blackest gloom. From inside the barn came the sounds of hammering. Shorty was building a crate to ship Shag east. Up at the house Ellen was finishing her packing. She and Charlie had both talked to his father, but he would not risk keeping the dog and allowing him to run loose. Charlie would drive Ellen to the station as soon as she was ready.

Charlie's hand dropped to Shag's head and his fingers moved over the healed scar on his neck. A frown formed on his lips. He looked closely at the scar. Several times he had thought Shag had gotten that wound fighting the old she-wolf. But that suggestion had not impressed Tex or his father. To Charlie's way of thinking, there was pretty good evidence in

175

Shag's favor. No one had sighted the wolf pack since the night of the kill, and there was the scar.

Charlie stirred and sat up very straight. A thought had suddenly hit him. It was a wild chance, but it was very simple. As he jumped to his feet, he wondered why he had never thought of it before. He dropped to his knees beside Shag.

"You and I are hitting for the hills," he said.

Shag's tail thumped the ground, but he did not lift his head. Charlie got to his feet. He stepped into the saddle house and got his gear. He headed for the corral at a fast trot.

Charlie led Trey Spot to where Shag was chained. He bent down and unfastened the chain. Shag got to his feet quickly. He cocked his head and looked up inquiringly at Charlie. Then he jumped up against him and whimpered eagerly.

"I've been a dumb cluck," Charlie said. He turned and swung into the saddle. "Come along, boy," he called to Shag as he headed Trey Spot out toward the big meadow. Shag bounded after the mare, staying behind until Charlie gave a wild whoop, then leaped ahead.

Shorty came out of the barn and stood with his hands on his hips. A look of mild astonishment formed on his face as he watched the black mare and her rider charge away across the meadow, with Shag racing ahead of them. Charlie's whoop floated back to him. He shook his head as he turned back to the barn. Grandby would be sore if Charlie didn't get back with the dog in time for Ellen to catch her train.

Charlie knew he was betting against long odds, but

the stakes were big and his hunch was a strong one. He headed straight out across the hay meadow toward the slopes where the calves were pastured. Shag was running with wild abandon. It was the first free run he had had in a long time.

They reached the calf pasture and headed up to the spot where the wolves had made their kill. When they reached the spot, Shag sniffed about. His neck scruff lifted and he growled. Charlie laughed.

"You can still smell wolf?" he asked.

The next step was to head Shag toward the woods. Charlie turned the mare toward the timber and watched the dog. Shag ran ahead with muzzle low. They entered the woods and Shag swerved toward a small clearing. He bounded to the center of the clearing and stood there, sniffing and growling. Charlie rode out to where the dog stood. What he saw lying in the tall grass made him leap from his saddle.

At his feet lay the remains of a big gray wolf. Shag looked up at Charlie and wagged his tail. He had waited a long time for the chance to show what he had done and to be rewarded.

"I'd sure like to have seen the fight," Charlie said. In spite of the condition of the body, it was clear that the wolf had died as the result of a slashed throat. Charlie laid a hand on the dog's head. "Good work, Shag," he said with feeling.

Shag wagged his tail furiously and leaped up against Charlie. Charlie laughed as he pushed the big fellow away from him. He was eager to get back to the ranch with the news. He mounted Trey Spot and turned her head toward home.

The ride back to the ranch was a wild one. Trey Spot caught the excitement and galloped after Shag as he sped down the slope and out across the hay meadow. They came charging around the big barn, with Shag barely clear of Trey Spot's pounding hoofs. Ellen was at the saddle house. His father was coming down the path with her bags. Shorty stood beside the pickup truck. Charlie grinned at Ellen as he hit the ground in front of her. Shag ran up to her and wagged his whole body in his eagerness.

"Put the truck away," Charlie called to Shorty.

"But I'll miss my train," Ellen protested.

"You're not going away," Charlie said.

His father stopped beside them and set Ellen's bags on the ground. "It was all right to have a last run with the dog," he said, "but you have to hurry."

"They're not going to leave." Charlie almost shouted the words. "Shag is innocent. In fact, he's a hero and we can prove it!"

Grandby and Shorty stared at Charlie. Ellen started to laugh excitedly. "How can you prove it?" she asked.

"Shag took me straight to the carcass of the old she-wolf he killed up there above the calf pasture."

"Oh, Charlie, this is wonderful news! Shag would never be happy anywhere but in the mountains."

"I've sure been dumb," Charlie said. "Letting Shag prove his innocence was the first thing we should have tried."

"This is the best news we've had in a long time." Grandby smiled broadly.

"Looks like we got us a sure-enough cow dog," Shorty commented.

At his feet lay the remains of a big gray wolf

Ellen turned and ran toward the house. Grandby picked up Ellen's bags and followed her. Charlie turned to Trey Spot. He cared for her, then went to see Golden Boy. It seemed natural to go to the stallion. Golden Boy was part of his life, and should share the good news. The big palomino charged across the corral and slid to a halt at the gate. Charlie watched him with a critical eye.

"This is the day when good things happen, big boy," Charlie said. "Takes a little faith to make things work out. When we make the big drive to trap Prince, I'll be riding you, and you'll come through."

Golden Boy tossed his head impatiently. Charlie grinned at him. Proving Shag's innocence had been so simple. He thought about Pedro. Trapping Seller into an admission should be simple. A glimmer of an idea began to form in Charlie's mind. The more he thought about the idea, the bigger it grew. He didn't have much time. Colby was taking Pedro to the reform school in a day or so. He was beating the idea around when Tex rode in.

As Tex unsaddled his horse at the corral gate he gave Charlie a cold look.

"Who turned that dog loose?" he asked.

"I did," Charlie said cheerfully. "From now on he has the run of the ranch."

"There've been some mighty fast changes made," Tex muttered.

"I took Shag out today and he led me to the carcass of the she-wolf he killed when she and her pack raided the calf pasture," Charlie explained.

Tex shrugged his shoulders. If Charlie said he had

seen the carcass of a wolf up there, Tex believed him. He also knew that Charlie could be right about the dog.

"Could be I was wrong," he said as he picked up his saddle.

Grandby came out of the barn and joined them. Charlie grinned at Tex. "We're all wrong at times. This has taught me a few things. I'm making one more try at trapping Seller."

"When?" Grandby asked.

"Tomorrow," Charlie answered.

"Would you care to let me in on your plan?" Grandby asked with a smile.

"It's so wild that I guess I'd better not," Charlie said, then added quickly, "But it's not dangerous."

Grandby was so relieved to have the dog trouble settled that he did not argue. Ellen's decision to go home had disturbed him greatly.

Charlie was eager to go to the house. He wanted to talk to Ellen. They could go for a ride in the hills. It had been quite a while since they had ridden together. When he reached the house, she was upstairs unpacking. He waited until she came down.

"I feel like taking a fast, hard ride. Want to come along?" he asked.

"Yes. A hard ride would be wonderful." Ellen laughed happily. "I'll run up and change my clothes."

Charlie watched her run up the stairs. He felt pretty good. Everything would be fine if Pedro weren't waiting in jail, facing a trip to the reform school.

15. A Test

CHARLIE'S PLAN for trapping Seller included Shag. He also needed the help of Sheriff Colby, and that was something he wasn't sure he could get. Sheriff Colby might be hard to persuade. In order to get it all done in one day he was up and away from the ranch by three o'clock in the morning. Shag was ready for a run and raced ahead of Trey Spot.

He had decided against leaving a note. Grandby would know he was off for a last try at Seller. He had not worn his gun, but he had brought along Shag's collar and leash. Golden Boy whinnied eagerly as they rode away.

Daylight found Charlie close to Cedar Bank. He would be too early to see the sheriff, so he decided to have breakfast in a Main Street café.

The sun was up when he halted at the hitch rack

in front of the café. Charlie put the collar on Shag and they started toward the café. When they entered, the man in back of the counter gave the dog a long look. Charlie grinned at him.

"Have to keep him with me," Charlie explained. "I wouldn't want him to eat up any of your town dogs."

"He looks like he could do it," the counterman said. "What'll you have?"

"Ham and eggs and coffee." Charlie looked down at Shag. "And two plain hamburgers."

As Charlie ate his ham and eggs and Shag bolted the two hamburgers, Charlie started worrying. Now that he was about to face Colby, his plan seemed wild and foolish, even to himself. He sat for a while thinking about it as he drank a second cup of coffee. Finally he paid his check and left.

He hoped Colby was an early riser. Rounding a corner, he saw that the jail door was open. When he looked into the jail office, he saw the sheriff seated at his desk. He had a cup of coffee in front of him and was smoking his pipe. He showed no surprise when he saw Charlie.

"Come in, Charlie. Just in time for coffee."

Charlie entered with Shag at his heels. He sat down beside the desk. Shag stretched out on the floor at his feet.

"I had a loco idea yesterday," Charlie began.

The sheriff smiled and waited.

"Is Seller up at the Dillon cabin?" Charlie asked.

The sheriff nodded. "You still after him?"

"I thought we could go up there. You could be looking for Dillon's money. Seller hates Shag, and he's

afraid of him. Dillon liked the dog. They were friends."
Charlie smiled.

Sheriff Colby puffed on his pipe and looked down
at Shag. He rubbed his stubbly chin with a thumb
and finger.

"Sure looks like a big gray wolf." He shook his head.
"How about that coffee?"

"No, thanks. We just came from the café." Charlie
wasn't going to let Colby sidetrack the issue. "I figure
Seller hated Dillon, but was afraid of him. They must
have had trouble; possibly Dillon fired Seller. Anyway, Seller shot Dillon with Pedro's gun. He must
have planned it well ahead because the gun was
missing for a week. He cut Dowd and Lester in to in-
sure an alibi."

"You figure to use the dog to make Seller break?"

"That's the idea. He's sure afraid of Shag."

"Do you think he'd believe a dog would remember
and want revenge?" Colby asked doubtfully.

"A guilty conscience might help," Charlie said
eagerly. "It would be worth a try."

Colby stood up and got a cup of coffee. As he sipped
it, he was thoughtful.

"You should have seen him the day Shag and I
visited the cabin. When he saw Shag he went white
as a ghost and started yelling at me to keep him
away." Charlie leaned forward eagerly.

"Can you control him?" Colby asked.

"He's well trained. I can handle him," Charlie said
confidently.

"Seller will be feeling safe. Pedro has been convicted." Colby smiled at Charlie. "And while we're

mentioning the boy, I want to say that I watched him closely at the trial. I believe he was telling the truth. I don't agree with Judge McHenry."

"Then it has to be Seller working with Dowd and Lester."

Colby nodded. "Dowd and Lester have pulled out. They had a row with Seller. I think it was over their spending so much money gambling. But I know where they are."

"You'll go along with my idea?" Charlie asked eagerly.

"We'll give it a try. No man has ever gotten away with murder in this county since I've been sheriff," Colby stated grimly.

"Thanks, Sheriff," Charlie said.

"You can go back and talk to Pedro while I get my horse and have a word with my deputy." Sheriff Colby got to his feet and handed Charlie the cell key.

Pedro was in his bunk with a blanket pulled up around his ears. When Charlie unlocked the cell door, he sat up.

"Hi, sleepyhead," Charlie greeted him.

Pedro ran a hand over his tousled black hair. He was surprised to see Charlie. "Is the sheriff ready?" he asked. "You didn't need to come in to see me off," he added.

"You're not going today," Charlie said. "The sheriff and I are paying Seller a visit. Now that he thinks he's safe he may have dug up the money." Charlie grinned. "We're taking Shag with us." He whistled and Shag came bounding down the hall. He skidded into the cell and leaped up against Pedro. Pedro pushed him down. He wasn't sure that he wanted to say good-by to the dog. It would have been easier if Charlie had not brought him in.

"You're getting fat," he said gruffly. "Not enough work out there for you."

"Too much of Mrs. Garrity's cooking," Charlie said.

Pedro turned to Charlie. "What good will it do to go out there?"

"If we find the money, Seller will have to explain how he got it."

"He'll say he found it where I hid it and was going to bring it in." Pedro wasn't cheered up at all.

"You look at the dark side," Charlie said. "We figure Shag may be able to persuade Seller a bit."

Pedro's eyes showed a glimmer of hope that faded at once. "He's afraid of Shag. He might shoot him."

"He won't do any shooting," Charlie said grimly.

Colby called out, "Ready to ride, Charlie?"

"Ready," Charlie called back. He turned to Pedro. "Keep your fingers crossed."

Pedro smiled at him. "I will not hope too much," he said.

Charlie closed and locked the cell door. He and Shag hurried out to where the sheriff stood with his deputy at the front door. Colby was strapping on his old single-action Colt.

"See that the boy gets a good hot dinner," he said to the deputy as he turned to his horse.

They walked to the rack where Trey Spot was hitched. Charlie unsnapped Shag's leash but left the collar in place. They mounted their horses and headed out of town. The sheriff was an old saddle hand, tough and hard. He let Charlie set the pace and did not object when Charlie made it a fast lope.

Hours later they crossed a ridge and dropped down into Willow Creek. They followed it up through the foothills and on to where its valley narrowed and mountains loomed on each side.

It was past noon when they sighted the clearing where the cabin stood. Seller's horse was picketed in a meadow above the cabin, and a thin spiral of smoke rose from the cabin chimney.

"Looks as if he's here," Colby said.

Shag began acting aggressive as they neared the cabin. His head was up and his neck scruff bristled. He looked very much like a wolf. Charlie grinned. Shag was playing his part well. Shag halted a few steps from the cabin door and waited for Charlie and the sheriff. The two men dismounted and stood looking at the closed door. Shag had caught Seller's scent and was growling. He, too, was looking at the door, his head cocked on one side.

"You ready?" Colby asked. He gave Shag a worried glance. "You sure you can handle him?"

Charlie nodded and laid a hand on Shag's head. The sheriff stepped to the door and rapped loudly. No one answered, but they could hear someone moving about in a hurried manner inside the cabin. The sheriff rapped again.

"Open up, Seller. This is the sheriff." Colby tried the door, but it was barred on the inside.

Boot heels rapped across the floor. The door opened a foot and Seller looked out. Colby's burly form hid Charlie and Shag from his view.

"Hello, Sheriff," Seller said as he swung the door slowly open. He seemed nervous and reluctant to ask the sheriff to enter the cabin.

"Thought I'd have a look around," Colby said gruffly. "I'm supposed to locate Dillon's money."

"It ain't here," Seller said quickly. "I've looked plenty, and if I'd found it, I'd have brought it in."

Colby looked down at two packed saddlebags just inside the door. "Leaving?" he asked.

"Just a trip into the hills. I spotted a herd of wild horses up there and aim to look them over." Seller continued to block the doorway. "I'm a bit late starting. I'll head on out and you can search the cabin." Seller started to reach for the saddlebags.

At that moment Shag snarled. Colby stepped aside and Seller saw the dog. Seller's eyes opened wide and he took a step backward. Shag crouched, his eyes fixed on Seller.

"Get that dog out of here!" Seller shouted. His hand dropped to the butt of his gun.

"Easy," Colby warned. He stepped inside the cabin and jerked Seller's gun from its holster. "You act nervous, so I'll take your gun to make sure nothing happens."

Seller stared at Shag, who was rumbling deep in his chest. Charlie placed a hand on the dog's shoulders.

"We had an idea the dog might smell out the hiding place where Dillon cached the money," Colby said smoothly. "The way he acts gives me the impression he really knows who shot Tom Dillon."

"Keep him away from me!" Seller's voice was high and unsteady. "He's a killer!"

Charlie spoke for the first time. "You can't fool a dog, Seller. He was Dillon's friend and he's Pedro's dog." Charlie removed his hand from Shag's shoulders. The dog moved forward, uncertain as to whether he had permission to leap at the man facing him. When Charlie did not say a word, Shag leaped straight at Seller's throat. Charlie caught hold of the dog's collar and pulled him back.

"Not yet, Shag," he said.

Seller screamed and stumbled backward. Shag remained rigid, his fangs bared. When Charlie released his grip on the collar, the dog edged forward in a half crouch.

"Are you going to talk or do I give him the word?" Charlie shouted.

Seller's mouth worked soundlessly. He could not take his eyes off the bared fangs and the foam-flecked lips of the dog. He had backed against the far wall of the cabin. Shag was slowly moving forward, waiting for a word from Charlie.

"I'll talk!" Seller screamed. "Take that brute away! He'll kill me!"

"Down, Shag," Charlie commanded. Shag sank to the floor, but he kept his eyes on Seller.

Colby's voice cut through the dusty air of the cabin. "You shot Dillon and stole his money. That right?"

Seller's eyes were on Shag. He acted like a man in

a trance. "I killed him," he said dully. "He was boot-
ing me out." His shoulders slumped, and he lifted a
hand to wipe sweat from his forehead. "I should have
killed the dog. He hated me because I put the boot
to him every time I got a chance."

Colby jerked a thumb toward a bench. "Sit down
before you fall down."

Seller sank on the bench. Colby stood looking down
at him. Shag's head moved and his eyes remained on
the man huddled on the bench. Seller stared sullenly
at the dog. He seemed to have come to a decision.

"You can't make this stick," he said. "Anybody
would admit anything with that dog at his throat."

Colby said nothing. He walked to the saddlebags
beside the door and started rummaging through them.
He finally found what he was looking for—a leather
case. He opened it and lifted out a bundle of papers
which he laid on the table. He next removed a thick
bundle of paper money tied with twine.

"How much did Dowd and Lester get?" he asked.

Seller maintained a sullen silence, but he did not
take his eyes off Shag.

"I'm bringing them in," Colby said. "I guess they'll
talk when they're faced with a murder rap." He
dropped the money back into the case and followed
it with the papers. "Anyway, this should be enough."
He shoved the leather case into his pocket. He pulled
out a set of handcuffs. Seller sat scowling at his wrists
while Colby snapped them on.

"I'll get his horse and saddle it," Charlie said.

"I won't move until he takes that dog away," Seller
whined.

Charlie stepped to the door. Shag got to his feet. He turned his back on the prisoner and trotted outside at Charlie's heels. Colby laughed as Shag disappeared.

"Smart wolf, that," he said.

Charlie saddled Seller's horse and led it to the cabin. Colby and his prisoner were outside the door. Seller mounted and sat staring down at Shag.

They rode up out of Willow Creek and over a ridge. Colby wanted to stop at a ranger station where there was a telephone. When they reached the station, he called the sheriff in the next county and asked him to arrest Dowd and Lester and bring them to Cedar Bank. Seller sat on his horse and listened to the call through the open door of the station.

Charlie kept grinning as they rode down off the ridge. He was elated, but Colby showed no excitement at all. The sheriff was convinced that he could have broken the case without Shag's help. He certainly would have searched the saddlebags. But he did have a confession, which he was sure Seller would repudiate once he got to a lawyer. However, he knew the ways of men like Seller, Dowd, and Lester. Once there was a break, each man would try to save himself.

It was five o'clock when they reached the jail. The deputy came out of the office and his eyes opened wide when he saw Seller with his wrists manacled.

"Got us a killer," Colby said. "Get Pedro out of the cell so I can lock this one up."

"I want a lawyer. You can't prove anything," Seller said sullenly after he had dismounted.

"Two witnesses heard you confess—me and Charlie." Colby smiled.

"You used the dog," Seller said, and scowled at Shag, who was on his best behavior toward the man he disliked.

"We'll bring the dog into court and prove he's gentle and harmless." Colby chuckled.

"I could turn state's evidence against Dowd and Lester. It was their idea to kill Dillon." Seller was losing his bravado.

"Can't promise you anything," Colby said. "Just go on in."

Pedro was in the office when they entered. His eyes were very bright as he watched the sheriff march Seller down the hall. Charlie grinned at him and Shag jumped up against him and tried to lick his face. Pedro was speechless and trembling.

Colby came back from locking Seller in the cell. He smiled at Pedro. "I'll call Judge McHenry and have a talk with him, then I think you can go home with Charlie."

The sheriff picked up the receiver on his wall phone and gave a number to the operator. Within a few minutes he was talking to Judge McHenry. He explained what had happened and the judge asked several questions. After considerable talk the sheriff hung up.

"It will take a little while to clear the record, but the judge says he'll turn you over to Charlie if you'll promise not to run away." Sheriff Colby seated himself at his desk and opened a drawer. He started laying out the few things he had taken from Pedro the day he entered the jail. Colby shoved them across the desk. "You'll have to stay at the Bar L. You'll be called as a witness against Seller, Dowd, and Lester."

"I'll be there," Pedro promised.

"We'll rustle you a horse at the stable," Charlie said.

Outside on the street Pedro halted and stood looking up at the mountains. He took a deep breath. "They never looked so good," he murmured softly.

"I'd like to surprise the folks, but we'll be late getting in. I guess we better call them," Charlie said.

They made the call from the stable while waiting for Pedro's horse. Ellen answered the phone.

"It's me—Charlie."

Instantly he knew Ellen had caught the excitement in his voice. She cried out eagerly:

"You found something!"

"I found a pint-size cow hand, and I'm bringing him home with me." Charlie almost shouted the words.

"Oh, Charlie!" Ellen's voice was shaking. He heard her turn and call to someone in the room. Then he heard his mother's voice and Grandby's. He had to talk to each of them. He pulled Pedro over beside him and Pedro tried to say something, but choked up and only managed a word or two. After they had hung up, Charlie laughed.

"They'll wait up for us. This will be some home-coming."

Pedro beamed and rubbed his shirt sleeve across his eyes. He was too full of emotion to say anything. The stableboy led his horse in. He glanced curiously at Pedro, having seen him at the trial, but he didn't ask questions.

The boys were five miles out of town before Charlie recalled that he hadn't eaten since breakfast. But he wasn't turning back. They'd have a real feed when they got home.

16. Big Show

EVERYONE was up and waiting when Charlie and Pedro arrived at the ranch. Even Tex and Shorty had stayed up. Shag announced their arrival by running ahead and barking loudly. For once the horses were neglected and left hitched at the front gate. Charlie dropped back and let Pedro take the lead.

Ann was the first to welcome him. When he stepped into the light from the porch, she met him and put her arms around him. "Welcome home," she cried.

Ellen took the hand Pedro shyly extended. He made a gallant attempt to bow to the women, but they had closed in on him too quickly. Shag leaped about and got into everybody's way.

Grandby slapped Pedro on the shoulder and Shorty shook hands with him. Tex looked uncomfortable, as though staying up was a sign of weakness, but he

195

managed a word of greeting before heading for the bunkhouse.

Mrs. Garrity, who had been in the kitchen preparing sandwiches, came down the steps with an agility hardly safe at her weight. She smothered Pedro in an embrace that made him wiggle free as fast as he could. She turned damp eyes on Shorty, and he decided that she was in a mood that could be dangerous. He hurried away to join Tex in the bunkhouse.

In the dining room Charlie told his story. Mrs. Garrity made Charlie promise not to start until she had the sandwiches, cake, and milk on the table and could sit down and listen. There was laughter when Charlie told about how Shag had terrified Seller.

"He's a terrible man," Charlie's mother said. She looked at Grandby. "Will they electrocute him?"

"I think not. I think he and the others will try to save their skins by talking," Grandby said.

Grandby smiled broadly at Pedro. "That white stallion of yours is ripe for picking. This calls for a celebration. Suppose we all ride up there tomorrow and trap him?"

"That would be a fine celebration," Pedro agreed happily.

"We better get right to bed, so that we can be up early." Ann Carter got to her feet.

"I'm going to eat three more sandwiches before I turn in," Charlie said. "This is the first food I've seen since breakfast."

Ann and Grandby went to their room, and Mrs. Garrity said good night and retired. Ellen sat with the boys while Charlie finished his sandwiches.

Charlie swallowed the last bite of the last sandwich and finished his milk. He smiled at Ellen.

"Faith is a wonderful thing." The words were for Ellen. Pedro looked from one to the other, a puzzled expression on his face.

Ellen smiled at Pedro. "Once or twice our faith weakened," she explained.

The boys said good night to Ellen and went to their room. Pedro looked outside to make sure Shag was all right. The big dog was lying on the door mat asleep.

The next morning everyone was up before dawn. Mrs. Garrity had a huge breakfast prepared. She was the only one who was not going on the expedition. No amount of excitement could induce Mrs. Garrity to get on a horse. Charlie, Ellen, and Pedro were to ride ahead and spot the herd. Tex and Shorty would trail in two pack horses loaded with a camp outfit and food for lunch and supper. No action was to be taken until Ann and Grandby arrived. They would travel slowly, but there was work to be done before the stampede could get under way.

Ellen rode Trey Spot, Pedro was mounted on Casey Jones, Charlie rode Golden Boy. Grandby frowned when he saw Charlie mount the stallion.

"Is he fit for a tough job like this one?" he asked.

Charlie smiled across at Ellen. He leaned forward and slapped the big palomino on the shoulder. "It's a matter of faith," he said. "I believe in Golden Boy. He has completely recovered—not a sign of a limp. We had a good workout this morning."

Grandby had caught the look that passed between

Ellen and Charlie. He shrugged his shoulders and said nothing.

"Golden Boy should be there," Ellen said. "It will be a victory for him."

Grandby nodded as he turned away. Pedro laughed. "To see the two big ones together again will be a great show."

Shag was bounding about, impatient to be off. Charlie kept a tight rein on Golden Boy, who was watching Casey Jones with a baleful eye.

"We're off," he said. "See you up at the breaks."

Grandby stood with Tex and Shorty, watching the three gallop away. Shorty's eyes followed the stallion. Golden Boy was swinging along with powerful strides, but his action was not what it should have been.

They crossed the home meadows and climbed into the foothills, avoiding Roaring River Canyon by taking a trail that detoured east and followed a long ridge. Charlie kept the pace down. He wanted the horses fresh when they reached the horse range.

The sun rose, and jackets came off to be tied behind their saddles. Golden Boy fought his bit and fretted more and more as they climbed higher. He took in deep draughts of the mountain air, searching for the scent of the mares.

When they reached the first rock formations at the lower edge of the breaks, Pedro whistled Shag back and ordered him to heel. He dropped in behind Casey Jones. Pedro glanced at Golden Boy.

"He will sound off when he smells the herd," he said with a smile.

Charlie laughed. "That means it will be up to you and Ellen to scout the herd and report to us at the trap."

Pedro drew himself up proudly. "We will be very careful," he said.

"I hope Prince is holding them where he usually does," Ellen said anxiously. "I'm so keyed up I'll die if we can't make the drive today."

Charlie left Ellen and Pedro in a stand of spruce. They rode upcountry; he rode in a wide circle that would bring him to the lower end of the trap. Golden Boy had a feeling that he was not heading toward his herd, and he gave Charlie a bad time for a mile or so, fighting his bit and threatening to buck.

When he reached the canyon where the trap was built, Charlie hitched Golden Boy securely to a spruce and climbed down for a look at the work to be done in closing the lower end of the trap. Poles had been stacked in a thicket, and posts lay waiting to be set in their holes. Charlie busied himself cleaning out the holes and dropping the posts into place, ready for tamping when Tex and Shorty arrived. He dragged poles from the pile and strung them next to the posts.

Everything was ready for tamping and spiking the posts into place when Tex and Shorty arrived with the pack horses. Shorty grinned eagerly as he surveyed what had been accomplished.

"Have her closed up in no time," he said.

They set to work and soon had the big posts tamped securely. The fence had to be high because the white stallion would try to leap over it, and it had to be strong. To give the fence more resistance the poles were spiked to the inside of the posts. The wild stallion would have to push over a post in order to loosen any of the poles. After the fence was finished, they busied themselves cutting willow boughs with which to camouflage the newly built barrier.

With the trap closed, they checked the heavy gate and attached ropes to spring it. The gate was built at an angle, so that its own weight would slam it shut once it was released. Green boughs were arranged to hide the man who would spring the trap.

The work finished, they sat in the shade and waited. Pedro and Ellen rode in, with Shag trailing Casey Jones. They dismounted and Charlie could tell by their smiles that everything was as they had hoped it would be.

"He is holding them in a meadow close to the canyon," Pedro reported. "He is one very cagey horse today."

Charlie turned to Shorty. "You're the horse expert. What is the strategy?"

"Most of us will come in in a circle from above. Plenty of noise and action, with Shag on their heels. At least one of us should be across the canyon, ready to head the big boy off if he tries to abandon the mares and climb out."

"Who springs the trap? Should we draw straws?" Charlie asked.

"I'll spring the trap," Tex said and smiled.

They all went to the spot well below the trap where the pack horses had been left. Shorty opened one of the packs and got out the lunch Mrs. Garrity had prepared. No campfire would be built until the drive was over, but Mrs. Garrity had fixed a gallon jug of hot coffee. Lunch was almost ready when Grandby and Ann Carter rode in. Ann was flushed and radiant. Grandby helped her down from her saddle.

"I'm hungry," she said as she seated herself.

Lunch was eaten rapidly. They all wanted to get going. Shorty explained the strategy, and ended with a warning.

"If he fights back and charges anyone, he's to be given a clear path. No use in trying to fight a horse like that."

Grandby nodded. "No one is to act foolishly," he cautioned. "I guess we all know what could happen." He looked at Charlie. "It would be folly to try to rope him."

Pedro looked solemnly up at Grandby. It was difficult for him to make such a promise, but he nodded his head.

Grandby picked the position across the canyon. Ann would ride with him. He felt that by having her away from the main drive, he could keep her from entering into the wild excitement of the chase. They left before the others so as to have time to ride slowly to their position.

Shorty, Pedro, Ellen, and Charlie, with Shag at heel, circled upward to get above the herd. They finally spotted the mares feeding in a meadow that was surrounded on three sides by heavy timber, the fourth being the rim of the canyon. They scattered out, with Ellen riding between Charlie and Pedro. The signal for the start of the drive was to be a shot fired by Shorty.

As they worked their way down through the timber, they spread out and rode slowly, trying to avoid loose rocks or dry limbs which might warn the white stallion of their approach. They knew that when Shorty reached the edge of the woods, he would halt and wait to make sure that they were all ready to break into the open at the same time. There was always the possibility that a vagrant breeze might carry their scent to the stallion and touch off the stampede prematurely, but they had to take that chance.

Charlie reached the edge of the wood and halted. After peering through the boughs a few minutes, he located the white stallion below him and to his left. That would place him close to the spot where Ellen would come out of the woods. He made ready and waited for Shorty's signal.

The shot rang out and Charlie sent Golden Boy charging into the open meadow. The big palomino had not caught the scent of the herd and he was startled by what he saw when he broke cover. The white stallion was as surprised as Golden Boy. His savage scream rang across the meadow and was answered by Golden Boy. It was clear that Prince sensed a trap. He hesitated and stood facing his charging rival. Charlie stood up in his stirrups and swung his rope. He realized that in his fury Golden Boy could not be restrained or guided. If the white stallion chose to fight, the two would crash together.

Charlie was aware of Ellen racing out of the woods and of Pedro, farther down, charging forward. He did not glance to the right to check on Shorty, but he saw Shag out in the meadow leaping toward the white stallion. He felt a desperate urge to throw his rope aside and jerk his carbine free. That would be the safe thing to do, the right thing. A bullet would stop the white stallion and prevent a crash which could be fatal to him and possibly to Golden Boy. But he did not drop the rope, he kept on swinging it and shouting as Prince screamed a final challenge and charged to meet Golden Boy.

There was no time to do anything but get set for the impact when the stallions' big bodies met. Suddenly Prince swerved and reared up, lashing out with his forefeet. Charlie had a glimpse of a gray form flying through the air, then Golden Boy was pivoting like a cat, shifting to meet the white challenger. But Prince had suddenly decided that he was in the midst of great danger. Mounted humans were closing in on him. His savage anger against Golden Boy gave way to his wild-horse instinct to get his herd away to safety. He charged toward the mares, bunched and watching, in the meadow below. Golden Boy raced after him with his ears laid back, his nostrils flaring. It was a test of speed, a powerful runner against a swift pacer. Golden Boy gained slowly, but the white stallion reached his herd and sent the mares plunging over the rim of the canyon before Golden Boy's teeth could reach the white rump just ahead of him. Charlie fought with all his strength to curb the big horse and to keep him from plunging over the rim after the fleeing horses. Golden Boy was not to be curbed. His rival was making off with the mares and had to be stopped.

Charlie glanced back before they took the plunge. In the meadow, Ellen had dismounted and was kneeling beside a gray form stretched out on the grass. That was all Charlie saw; he did not see Pedro or Shorty. Golden Boy leaped and slid and lunged down the deeply furrowed bank. He hit the bottom and shook himself, then charged away after the fleeing herd. Prince now had a considerable lead, but he was slowed because he had to lash at the lagging mares. Golden Boy was fast closing the gap when Charlie saw the trap ahead. The mares poured into it with the white stallion pushing them hard.

The danger now was that Golden Boy would plunge into the trap and battle the white stallion inside the small enclosure. Charlie jerked and sawed savagely. Blood reddened the foam on Golden Boy's muzzle, but he could not be slowed down. Suddenly Charlie saw the gate start to swing over and down. He got set to dive from the saddle. No one would be fool enough to ride into the corral on a stallion gone stark mad. The gate swung faster and dropped into place. Golden Boy saw it, and instinct saved him. He was very familiar with pole fences. He planted his feet and hit the gate at slackened speed. It sagged, but it held.

Golden Boy reared up and lashed at the bars. His scream rose above that of the white stallion and the frenzied whinnying of the mares and their colts and fillies. Charlie heard Tex shouting at him:

"Unload. Get off that horse!"

Then Pedro was beside him, forcing Casey Jones in close, and Charlie unloaded as he would off a bucking horse at a rodeo, swinging on behind Pedro. Pedro backed Casey Jones away and they watched Golden

"Unload! Get off that horse!" Tex shouted to Charlie

Boy and Prince lash at one another through the corral bars. Neither could do any damage, but both were filled with wild fury.

"Is Shag badly hurt?" Charlie had to raise his voice almost to a shout.

"I do not know," Pedro answered. "I saw that you could not control Golden Boy, so I came on to help you."

"We better go up and see," Charlie said. Shorty was riding down to the gate. He and Tex could do all that could be done at the trap.

Pedro turned Casey Jones around and they started up the canyon. They had gone only a few yards when Charlie saw Trey Spot on the rim above. Beside her stood Shag, his jaws parted, his tongue working over his fangs happily.

The mares had quieted down—a corral was natural to them. Prince and Golden Boy had fought themselves out and Charlie was able to lead the big palomino up out of the canyon and hitch him to a tree. Shorty had a fire pit built and Ann and Ellen were busily preparing a hot supper. Shag and Pedro sat on a ledge looking down at the big white horse in the corral. Everyone was relaxed, drained of energy by the excitement. Charlie sat beside his father, watching Ellen and his mother.

"I wonder what Pedro will do with the white stallion?" Charlie asked.

"I believe he plans to sell him," Grandby answered. "If he does, I know the man who will buy him. He'll be out from the East this fall. But why don't you ask him?"

"Good idea." Charlie got to his feet and walked down to the ledge where Pedro and Shag were seated. Pedro looked up and smiled.

"I have been studying him," he said. "He could never be trusted as a range stallion, but he would make a great show horse."

"What do you plan to do with him?" Charlie asked.

"I should not take him. He should belong to your father or to you," Pedro answered gravely.

"He's yours, and if you want to sell him, Dad has a buyer he says will pay a big price for him."

"I have watched him for an hour," Pedro said. "I will trade him to your father for Casey Jones, who is my friend and will always do as I wish. The white one would never be a real friend."

Charlie smiled, but as he watched the white horse, he had a feeling that Pedro was right. Prince was a very smart horse, smarter perhaps than Golden Boy, but he had the manners and the look of an unpredictable animal.

"At the moment I agree," Charlie said. "But he may change when Shorty starts working him."

"He'll never change." Pedro was positive. He was depending upon a sixth sense he had with horses which had never failed him.

Charlie nodded agreement. Pedro turned to face him.

"There are a few things I want to tell you," he said. "I have learned a lot living here with you and your folks and Ellen. I do have a family. We lived in Mexico and were always poor. There were so many of us —ten children. We moved to New Mexico and we were still poor. I learned to do a man's work when I was ten."

"You learned about horses?"

Pedro nodded. "It was always horses. I thought that if I left home, it would be easier for my father." Pedro's eyes were following the white stallion. "I would make much money and send some home. I had worked for a man and he had given me a horse and a saddle. That was the horse Dillon sold."

Charlie waited, saying nothing. Pedro reached down and patted Shag's head before he went on talking.

"Judge McHenry says I will get my third of the Dillon money and also the money Dillon got for my horse. Your father will send most of it home for me."

Charlie's mother called to them. Supper was ready. They joined the others around the campfire. Grandby Carter moved over beside Charlie. Pedro and Shag sat across the fire with Ellen.

"Is Pedro going to sell the horse?" Grandby asked.

Charlie grinned. "He's trading him to you for Casey Jones."

His father chuckled. "I knew Pedro and that roan had struck up a real friendship. I was going to give the horse to him, but I'll accept the trade, and when the stallion is sold, I'll split the money with Pedro."

Pedro had filled his tin plate. He did not return to where Ellen was sitting but came and sat down beside Charlie. Shag stretched out at his feet. The dog had been shaken up badly when Prince tossed him. He wasn't feeling very frolicsome. Charlie reached down and stroked the dog's head.

"He turned Prince," Charlie said slowly. "I guess that saved me from a bad mess."

"He attacked as he does an angry bull," Pedro said proudly. "He is afraid of nothing."

"He's a great dog," Grandby agreed. "We saw everything he did."

Pedro looked up at Grandby. "I would like to stay and work awhile on the Bar L. I would like to help handle the white one."

"We can use both you and Shag at a proper salary," Grandby said quickly.

"I do not need much pay," Pedro answered. "Charlie says the stallion is mine." He waited for Grandby's answer.

"That's right. You saw him first and were after him. We just helped you catch him." Grandby smiled.

"I will trade him to you for Casey Jones." Pedro watched Grandby's face anxiously.

"It's a deal," Grandby said. "But if I sell him and he brings more than Casey Jones is worth, we'll split the amount left over."

Pedro beamed. He had been worrying a little for fear Grandby might not want to trade.

With supper over, Tex and Shorty prepared for an overnight camp. Pedro decided to stay with them. The others would ride back to the ranch. The men would have the job of releasing the mares without letting Prince escape, and of holding them until Charlie brought Golden Boy back to take over as range stallion. He and Ellen would return with an extra horse for Charlie to ride after he had released Golden Boy.

Charlie and Ellen rode on ahead, setting a much faster pace than Grandby would let his wife ride. They rode close together, content just to feel the mountains around them, and to enjoy the sunset and the coming dusk. When they were crossing the home meadow, Ellen said:

"This has been a beautiful summer."

Charlie wanted to say a lot of things to the girl riding beside him, but all he managed was a brief word —"Swell."

At the house Mrs. Garrity was bustling with excitement. They were hardly inside the door when she started telling them the news.

"Sheriff Colby called and left a message. That man Seller gave him a signed confession, and he has the other two men locked up. He said to tell Pedro he is a free man." She looked past them and out through the screen door. "Is Shorty sleeping out tonight?"

"He is," Charlie said and smiled.

"And with him complaining of an ache in his back." Mrs. Garrity frowned and headed for the kitchen.

Charlie smiled down at Ellen. "Big day tomorrow."